W9-AUZ-306

after

Kristin Harmel

after

DELACORTE PRESS

This is a work of fiction. Names, characters, places, and incidents either are the product of the author's imagination or are used fictitiously. Any resemblance to actual persons, living or dead, events, or locales is entirely coincidental.

 Published in the United States by Delacorte Press, an imprint of Random House Children's Books, a division of Random House, Inc., New York.

Delacorte Press is a registered trademark and the colophon is a trademark of Random House, Inc.

Visit us on the Web! www.randomhouse.com/teens

Educators and librarians, for a variety of teaching tools, visit us at www.randomhouse.com/teachers

Library of Congress Cataloging-in-Publication Data
Harmel, Kristin.
After / Kristin Harmel. — 1st ed.
p. cm.
Summary: When her father is killed in a car accident, Lacey feels responsible, so when she is given a chance to make a difference in the lives of some of her fellow students, she jumps at the chance.
ISBN 978-0-385-73476-9 (hardcover) — ISBN 978-0-385-90475-9 (lib. bdg.) — ISBN 978-0-375-89488-6 (e-book)
[1. Grief—Fiction. 2. Guilt—Fiction. 3. Family life—Fiction. 4. High schools—Fiction. 5. Schools—Fiction.] I. Title.
PZ7.H2116Af 2010
[Fic]—dc22
2009001367

The text of this book is set in 12-point Garamond BE.

Book design by Angela Carlino

Printed in the United States of America

10 9 8 7 6 5 4 3 2 1

First Edition

To my friends Kate Atwood, Carleigh Pearson,
Cole Pearson, Luke Pearson, and everyone else
who has lost a parent too soon.

• • •

And as always, to Carol Harmel.
I couldn't ask for a better mother.
I love you!

A BIG THANK-YOU

To Kate Atwood, the founder of Kate's Club in Atlanta, and to NFL quarterback Brian Griese, the founder of Judi's House in Denver. Both of you lost a parent too soon, and you've turned your grief into something that has helped thousands of children. Your mothers would be so very proud of you. I'm honored to have become a part of your world.

To the Pearsons: Susan, Carleigh, Cole, and Luke. This book, while not based on you, was inspired by the time I've spent with you. I'm so glad to call you friends; I feel like you're my Atlanta family! And I'm so impressed with all of you; you're all amazing, strong, kind people, and I can't wait to see what wonderful things life brings you.

To my wonderful editor, Wendy Loggia, who has once again helped beat a rough manuscript into shape. Your guidance is invaluable, and I'm glad to work with you.

To my amazing literary agent, Jenny Bent; her assistant, Chris Kondrich; my film agent, Andy Cohen; and the wonderful Delacorte Press family, including Elizabeth Zajac, Krista Vitola, and Angela Carlino.

To my *People* magazine editor, Nancy Jeffrey, who allows me to work on the kind of stories that inspire me, move me, and let me share the heroism of good people with the world.

To my own family, especially Mom, Dad, Karen, and Dave, and to all my wonderful friends.

To all of my many writer friends: It's such a pleasure and honor to know all of you. Thanks especially to Megan Crane, Liza Palmer, Jane Porter, Melissa Senate, Sarah Mlynowski, Alison Pace, Lynda Curnyn, Brenda Janowitz, Lisa Daily, and Emily Giffin, who are truly wonderful people as well as wonderful writers.

And to you, the reader. This book is about changing your own little corner of the world. I hope that you feel inspired. Thanks for reading!

after

prologue

The day my whole world changed started like any other Saturday.

"Lacey!" my dad called. "Are you coming? It's going to be dinnertime when we get there!"

I looked in the bathroom mirror and made a face. He said the same thing every Saturday morning–but maybe that was because I took longer getting ready than anyone else.

"Why don't you just get up earlier?" My brother Logan, who was eleven months older than me, appeared in the doorway and looked suspiciously at my reflection. I knew he'd been sent up to get me. I was putting on a coat of mascara and paused to glare at him.

"I need my beauty sleep," I said, trying to sound haughty.

He rolled his eyes. "No kidding," he muttered. "I think you need a little more."

He was gone by the time I threw a tube of toothpaste at him.

Five minutes later, when I came downstairs, my dad, Logan, and my little brother, Tanner, were standing in the hallway, already bundled up in their coats and scarves. It was unusually cold that day, even though it was only November fifteenth. There had been an early freeze, and it hadn't worn off yet. My dad held out my pink puffer jacket, and as I stepped into the hallway and took it from him, he winked, one corner of his mouth jerking upward just a little. I knew he was trying to hide his amusement from Logan and Tanner.

"What the heck takes you so long anyway?" Tanner said. "I'm glad I'm not a girl."

Logan high-fived him. My dad looked up at me. "Is Your Royal Highness finally ready?" he asked, bowing slightly.

My dad always called me that when I took a long time to get dressed. Even though he sometimes pretended to be as exasperated as Logan and Tanner, I think he secretly didn't mind.

"Where's my beautiful wife?" Dad singsonged as I zipped up my jacket. Mom rounded the corner, dressed in the same ratty pink bathrobe she'd had for years, the one she would never throw away because it was the first gift Logan and I ever picked out for her, when Logan was four and I was three and Dad took us Christmas shopping. We'd bought her a new one last Christmas, but she refused to switch over.

She was in her usual state of morning messiness, with sleep-flattened reddish brown, shoulder-length curls flying every which way and her cheeks slightly blotchy before she made it to her vanity mirror and her tray full of makeup. I always wished that I had inherited her pretty hair and Dad's flawless complexion, but instead, it was the other way around. I had Dad's stick-straight dirty blond hair that always looked stringy if I didn't use a curling iron on the ends (which I hardly ever had time to do considering I shared a bathroom with two boys) and Mom's acne-prone skin. Thank goodness for Clearasil, but most of the time my face was sporting at least one major zit, usually in a totally unflattering location like the middle of my forehead or smack in the center of my chin.

"You're taking my family and leaving me?" Mom asked dramatically, clutching her hands over her heart. "Whatever will I do?"

Mom said the same thing every Saturday when Dad took the three of us out to breakfast. He called it "Dad time," and while we were out scarfing down pancakes at the Plymouth Diner, Mom was having her weekly "Mom time," which apparently included sitting around in her robe, sipping a cup of coffee, and putting on a facial mask while she fast-forwarded through TiVoed episodes of *Grey's Anatomy* and *CSI* and whatever else she'd dozed off watching during the previous week.

"Your mom thinks we're giving her time alone," Dad would whisper to us while she pretended she couldn't hear, "but really, it's just a good excuse for the four of us to hang out and eat greasy bacon and hash browns, right?"

It had been our Saturday-morning routine for as long as I could remember. And it was the highlight of every week. Dad, Logan, Tanner, and I would sit at breakfast and talk about school and our friends and stuff, and Tanner, who wanted to be a comedian when he grew up, would always tell some silly joke he had just learned from his friends or the Internet that week, and when we'd get home, the house would always be a little cleaner, and Mom was always in a good mood. If we didn't have anything big to do, we'd all go out for a hike or a bike ride or to play tennis at the local country club, where Mom had insisted we needed a membership, against Dad's halfhearted protests.

Mom and Dad kissed goodbye, then she gave each of us a peck on the top of our heads, and we were off.

"Everyone have their seat belts on?" Dad asked as he started the car. Logan climbed in beside him.

"Yes!" the three of us answered in unison. Dad turned and grinned at Tanner and me in the back, buckled his own seat belt, and put the car in reverse. As we pulled out of the driveway, he beeped the horn at Mom and blew her a kiss.

"Cheesy!" Logan and I chorused. Tanner laughed.

Mom smiled, waved from the doorway, and went inside.

It took three minutes for us to get out of our neighborhood, Plymouth Heights, and onto a main street. It's weird how normal everything still was in those final minutes. We saw Mrs. Daniels walking down her driveway to pick up the newspaper, and she waved at us as we passed. Dad and Logan waved back. I noticed Jay Cash and Anne Franklin, two kids from Tanner's grade, playing basketball in the Cashes' driveway. Anne tripped on her shoelace just before we passed, and I turned my head slightly to see if she'd start crying. She didn't. Logan was absorbed in flipping through the radio stations, finally settling on the classic-rock station, which was playing the Eagles' "Hotel California," one of Dad's favorite songs. He started to sing along, and when the chorus ended and a guitar solo began, Dad glanced at Tanner and me in the rearview mirror and grinned.

"You guys would love California," he said. "Maybe we'll go there someday and surf."

"I want to surf!" Tanner exclaimed. At age eleven, he had just discovered skateboarding, and he had announced more than once at dinner that when he turned eighteen, he was going to move west, bleach his hair blond, and learn to catch waves. I had to admit, it was a fun fantasy to have in the middle of a Massachusetts winter.

"I know!" Dad laughed as the light on Mayflower Avenue turned green and he eased his foot off the brake and onto the gas. He put on a fake surfer accent. "Hang ten, dudes!"

It was the last thing Dad ever said.

I think I saw it an instant before it happened, but my throat closed up, and there wasn't time to open my mouth or even to scream before the Suburban plowed into the driver's side of the car, hitting us with such force that the whole side crumpled, pinning me up against Dad's seat. It was like everything was suddenly compressed into a much smaller space than it had been a second ago. I felt a terrible pain along the left side of my body, shooting from my upper leg, up my side, and down my shoulder into my arm. I screamed and felt Tanner grope for my right arm.

The world felt dark and hazy. I couldn't see anything, just shapes, and everything sounded muffled. I wondered for a second if I was dying. Far away, I could hear Logan yelling and Tanner crying. But I couldn't hear Dad. Why couldn't I hear Dad?

My throat felt like I'd swallowed cotton balls, and my mouth wasn't responding when I tried to make it work. I opened and closed it a few times, but I was only gurgling, not talking. I remember being terrified, and when I look back now, I think it was pure fear that kept me from being able to speak. When I finally did, there was only one thing that came out of my mouth.

"Daddy?" I whispered weakly. I hadn't called him that since I was twelve.

It was the last thing I remember saying before everything went black.

• • •

When I came to, I was in the hospital. I didn't know how much time had passed. But I think I already knew about Dad. I don't know how–I didn't see him again after the Suburban hit us–but maybe when you're that close to someone, you can feel it when they're not there anymore. That's what I think, anyhow.

It took me a few moments to focus on Mom's face as I gradually swam to the surface of consciousness. Her eyes were bloodshot and her face was blotchier than usual. I couldn't help noticing that she was still wearing the tattered pink bathrobe over her pajamas, which seemed strange and out of place in public. Mom was a lawyer in Boston, and she never left the house looking anything less than completely put-together.

The hospital room was white and almost uncomfortably bright under big fluorescent lights. I licked my lips and realized I couldn't feel my body.

Mom jumped up and leaned over me. She looked scared.

"You're going to be okay," she blurted out. "You broke your left femur–that's the big bone in your thigh–in two places, and you have a few broken ribs and a broken left wrist, but they say all the bones should heal just fine."

"Where's Dad?" I asked slowly, in a voice that sounded too thick to be my own.

Mom's lower lip quivered and she bit it, like it was the only way she could stop it from shaking. Her eyes filled with tears again.

"Lacey, baby," she said softly, sitting on the edge of my bed and reaching for my hands. I couldn't feel her. I couldn't feel anything. "The accident was really bad."

I stared at her for a minute. She hadn't answered me. "Where's Dad?" I repeated. "Where are Tanner and Logan?"

She blinked at me a few times. "The boys are in the waiting room," she said. "Uncle Paul's with them. They're going to be okay. Tanner broke his arm, and Logan had to get stitches, but they're fine."

I remembered Tanner reaching for me just before everything went black. He must have been scared about me. "But Dad?" I asked again, my voice rising a little bit as panic began to set in.

"Dad . . . ," Mom began, and then stopped. She took a big breath, glanced away, and then looked back at me with eyes that seemed foggy and lost. "The car . . . hit right around the driver's seat," she said slowly. "The doctors did everything they could, but . . ." She stopped, unable to say it.

"Daddy died," I completed her sentence, feeling tears well up in my eyes. "He died, didn't he?"

Mom nodded. A pair of fresh tears rolled down her face, one for each cheek, like skiers racing to the bottom of the slopes. I remembered the last thing Dad had said, and tried to imagine her tears as graceful surfers instead, trying to ride a wave into shore. But then the tears dropped off her jawline and melted into her robe, and I had the sudden feeling that the imaginary surfers had fallen off the edge of the wave and disappeared forever. It was that image that finally made me burst into tears.

Mom wrapped her arms around me, and we sobbed together, with no more words to say.

Later, after Logan and Tanner had come in to see me and Uncle Paul had taken them home, Mom sat by my bedside and told me that Dad had lost consciousness right away. The doctors said he probably didn't even see it coming and didn't feel scared, and that he was never awake to hurt. It was, they told her, the most painless way to go. One second, he was driving along happily on a Saturday morning with his three kids, and the next, it was all over. He never knew. He never had a chance to say goodbye.

After a while, Mom asked if I had any questions. I said no, but of course, that was a lie.

I wanted to ask what would have happened if I hadn't had to curl my hair or if I hadn't insisted on putting on mascara or if I hadn't purposely dragged my feet a little just to annoy Logan and Tanner. But I didn't need to ask. I knew what would have happened. We'd be sitting at home right now, trying to figure out whether to play Monopoly or Life or whether to watch a movie. Dad would be trailing his hand lazily down Mom's back in that affectionate way that sometimes made me and Logan smile and roll our eyes at each other. Mom would be getting up every few minutes to put dishes in the dishwasher or to start the washing machine. Logan and Tanner would be fighting over the remote control because Tanner wanted to watch a Pokémon DVD and Logan wanted to watch sports.

Dad wouldn't be dead.

And it wouldn't be my fault.

chapter 1

TEN MONTHS LATER

"And then I told Willow that her shoes were totally the wrong color for that outfit and actually, the shirt is really hideous anyhow, and I couldn't believe she was going to actually go out in that, never mind go to the movies with me, and then Melixa said to me . . ."

Sydney droned on and on from the front seat as I tried in vain to tune her out. Her high-pitched, squeaky voice made that pretty impossible, though. My best friend, Jennica, and I had decided that she must be trying to attract boys by sounding like a squeak toy, but until recently, I'd been sure that it only attracted dogs and whales and whatever else could hear such a high frequency.

But then she landed Logan, who apparently found squeakiness enticing. This pretty much meant that I was stuck with her, because she was now our official ride to school. Mom had refused to let me or Logan take our driver's tests since the accident, so it was either the school bus or hitching a ride with Logan's popularity-obsessed girlfriend.

"Uh-huh," Logan said patiently from the passenger seat, as if he were actually listening. As far as I could tell, Sydney was telling the longest story in the world about a bunch of senior cheerleaders who didn't matter to me at all.

"So what do you think?" Sydney finally paused for what I was pretty sure was the first breath she had taken since picking us up ten minutes ago.

"Um . . . ," Logan began, his voice trailing off. I hid a smile. He obviously hadn't been listening either. I watched in amusement as he struggled for words. "What do I think?" he said finally. "I think you're the most beautiful girlfriend in the world."

Oh, gag me. I waited for Sydney to realize that he was completely copping out, but instead she giggled, turned a weird shade of pink, and glanced at me in the rearview.

"What do *you* think, Lacey?" she asked. "Don't you think Summer was acting totally slutty? I mean, considering she's practically engaged to Rob Macavey?"

I sighed. "I don't even really know her."

"*Everyone* knows Summer Andrews," Sydney said, looking at me like I was a mental patient.

"Right." I bit my tongue. What I wanted to say was that everyone knew who Summer Andrews *was*—the cheerleading, BMW-driving, shiny-haired queen bee of our school—but that there were few people she actually deigned to talk to. And I was not one of them. I was pretty popular in my own grade, but I was definitely more bookworm than beauty-pageant contestant, which meant that Summer and her crowd hardly knew I was alive.

Logan was a different story. Since he and social-climbing Sydney had begun dating six months ago, he had come home more than once proudly reporting—out of Mom's earshot, of course—that he'd gotten drunk alongside Summer Andrews and her clones, Willow and Melixa, at parties. Like that was some major accomplishment.

But I refrained from saying any of this, because Logan would kill me if I did. He always seemed to be walking on thin ice around Sydney. I must have been making a face without meaning to, though, because Sydney glanced at me once more in the rearview and snorted.

"Oh come *on,* Lacey," she said. "Just because you're too busy making straight As and going to student council meetings and whatever else you think is so important doesn't mean that the rest of us can't have a social life."

I simmered for a minute. I was good at shutting my mouth, pressing my feelings into a little lockbox inside, and turning the key. I took a deep breath, blinked a few times, and said, "Wow, look at that! We're here already!"

Before either of them could respond, I hopped out of the car and began striding across the junior lot toward the school building without bothering to look back. Somewhere behind me, Sydney was babbling about how she couldn't believe I'd jumped out of her car before she'd even had a chance to park.

• • •

It was the end of the third week of school, and already, it seemed to have turned to fall. Last summer, the heat had hung on for ages, taunting us cruelly from outside the classroom windows with persistent rays of sunshine. But this year, the New England dreariness had moved in early, bringing hulking gray clouds and winds with a chilly edge. The first leaves on the trees were turning, seemingly overnight, from muted greens to the deep reds, oranges, and golden yellows that always reminded me of a sunset. I wasn't ready for it to be autumn again, but the seasons seemed to march on without caring.

Forty-five minutes after hopping out of Sydney's car, I was in trig class, trying to pay attention, which was hard to do considering that Jennica, who sat beside me, kept trying to get my attention. I was attempting to ignore her.

Math came easily to me. I had always wanted to be an architect when I grew up, like my dad. Plus, there was something about the clear-cut right and wrong of math equations that I found appealing. In math, there were no gray areas. There were rules, and I'd discovered that when you stayed inside the lines, life made a lot more sense.

"Psst!" Jennica hissed. I glanced to my right, where she had angled her desk closer to mine and was holding out a folded square of paper.

I glanced to the front of the room, where Mrs. Bost, our twentysomething teacher, was jotting a series of cosine problems on the board. In the few weeks we'd been in school, I'd already discovered that she had superhuman hearing. I suspected she could hear a note unfolding from miles away. So I coughed loudly to cover up the crinkling sound as I quickly unfolded Jennica's message.

You'll never believe this: Brian told me he LOVES ME last night! she'd written. I could feel Jennica's eyes on my face, so I was careful not to do anything inappropriate like, say, wrinkle my nose or stick out my tongue. It wasn't that I didn't like Brian. He was okay. But he and Jennica were so lovey-dovey with each other that I felt nauseated half the time I was around them. And much as I hated to admit it, I was a little jealous. *I* was the one Jennica had done everything with and told all her secrets to since we met in the first grade. And now Brian was her constant companion, and I felt like the third wheel.

It was like I'd lost my best friend. But it was selfish to feel that way, so I told myself not to. I'd gotten good at deciding how I should and shouldn't feel. Sometimes I felt like the director of the movie of my own life, yelling *action* in my head and then setting scenes in motion the way I'd decided they'd go.

I pulled out my cell phone, checked to make sure Mrs. Bost wasn't looking, and quietly texted Jennica: great. I watched as she silently pulled her cell from her purse, read my text, and frowned. She thought for a second, and I tried to tune back in to Mrs. Bost while Jennica typed. But the lecture was boring, and I was tired of thinking about trig and boyfriends and all the other dumb stuff that went along with eleventh grade. I was itching to graduate and get out of this place, to move on to the next phase of my life and leave Plymouth East behind, but I had a year and nine more months to go. It was endless.

The new-message indicator lit up on my phone. i know u've never been in love b4 but this is a REALLY BIG DEAL, Jennica had written, complete with a smiley face at the end of the sentence, to let me know she wasn't trying to be mean. Still, the words stung. I *knew* it was a big deal to her. But in my world, having a boy tell you he loved you wasn't exactly as earth-shattering as, say, your dad dying. it was when we were watching grey's antmy on dvd, the message continued. mcdrmy told mrdth he luved her & B turned 2 me & said, I luv u like derek luvs mer. sooo romantic, right?

I was just about to write something back when the door to the classroom creaked open. Mr. Dorsett, the assistant principal, was standing there with someone behind him. Mrs. Bost smiled and set down the marker she'd been using.

"I'm sorry to bother you," Mr. Dorsett said. He glanced over the room and then back at Mrs. Bost. "But we have a late addition to your class."

Twenty-four pairs of eyes strained to see the tall guy in a faded leather jacket and dark jeans who followed Mr. Dorsett through the doorway, his eyes focused coolly above our heads. His hair was dark, and it looked like he needed a haircut—or at least a comb. It stuck up wildly in some places and grazed his collar in others, making him look a bit like a mad scientist who forgot to go to the barber. His skin was tan, which made his pale green, thick-lashed eyes seem unusually bright.

A buzz went around the classroom. Plymouth was a pretty small town, and most of us had gone to elementary school or junior high together, so it wasn't very often that we saw an unfamiliar face. Maybe he'd transferred from the Catholic high school. Sometimes we got new students from there.

"Who's that?" Jennica whispered urgently, like everyone else in the room wasn't wondering the same thing. I shrugged without taking my eyes off the guy. I didn't usually notice things like this, but his eyes were unbelievable. They were almost the exact color of the ocean right before a storm. That had always been my favorite time to gaze out from the shore, while the wind whipped through my hair and the sky rumbled, getting ready to change the earth below it.

While Mr. Dorsett held an inaudible conversation with Mrs. Bost, the new guy shifted from foot to foot and avoided looking at anyone. I couldn't figure out whether he thought he was too cool for us or whether he was just nervous.

"Okay," Mrs. Bost finally began, pulling away from Mr. Dorsett. He nodded once at us, clapped the new guy on the back awkwardly, and headed out the door.

"This is Samuel Stone," Mrs. Bost continued once Mr. Dorsett was gone. "He'll be joining our class. I'd like you all to give him a warm welcome."

Jennica and I exchanged glances. The room was silent for a few seconds, then someone in the back started clapping slowly, and the rest of the class joined in. The new guy took a step forward and whispered something to Mrs. Bost.

"What?" she asked. She glanced at us. "Class! Shhh!"

We all quieted down in time to hear him say more loudly, "Sam."

All eyes were on the new guy, and suddenly I felt bad for him. I knew what that felt like. I'd been the subject of the same kinds of stares last fall, when I finally returned to school after the accident. It was the worst kind of attention; no one says anything; they just look and look, judging you. I blinked, cleared my throat, and shifted my gaze to the floor.

"Sam," he repeated, his voice sounding deeper than I'd expected it to. "I go by Sam."

"Oh," Mrs. Bost said. "I'm sorry. Welcome, Sam. There's an empty desk there, next to Lacey. Lacey, can you raise your hand?"

I looked up, startled. There seemed to be little need for me to put my hand in the air since Mrs. Bost was pointing straight at me, but I did anyhow, feeling my cheeks heat up as I did.

Sam began weaving through the rows full of students, who continued to stare like he was some kind of science project. I couldn't blame them. Not only was he new, but he was gorgeous. I mean, *really* gorgeous.

"Hey," he said, settling into the seat next to mine.

"Hey," I replied. He scooted his desk closer to mine so that he could see my book, and as he leaned over to glance at the text, I could feel his warm breath on my arm. I looked up and was surprised to find him studying me.

His eyes locked with mine. I shifted my gaze down and fumbled with my book. When I snuck another glance, he was still looking at me.

And for the first time since I'd seen him, Sam Stone cracked a small smile, and I felt a little tingle run up my spine. I smiled shyly back and looked away.

chapter 2

Sam Stone wound up in my sixth-period AP English class, too, and when he walked through the door and noticed me, he shot me a relieved look.

"Hey," he said, slipping into the empty seat beside me after yet another awkward, lengthy teacher introduction. "You're in this class too."

It was the longest sentence I'd heard him speak all day. I merely nodded, wondering why I seemed incapable of stringing words together.

"Lacey, right?" Sam asked, cracking another smile.

"Yeah," I said, my cheeks pinking.

"Cool name," he said, and for the first time, I noticed he had dimples. Not normal dimples, but almost vertical indentations along his cheeks, lines that made his face appear like it had been sculpted quite carefully by a really talented artist. "I'm Sam."

"I know." I didn't know what else to say, so I didn't say anything. He probably thought I was rude. Or maybe just dumb. I wasn't sure which was worse.

Jennica came home with me after school to study for our trig quiz on Friday. Sydney and Logan were going to some homecoming planning committee meeting, so Jennica and I had to take the bus. She didn't have a car either, although she had a license, and her mom let her borrow her car sometimes on the weekends.

"How come you're so good at this, and I'm so terrible?" Jennica grumbled as we sat down at the kitchen table and cracked our math books. Mom, who seemed to work 24-7, was still at the office, and Tanner had come home minutes after us and locked himself in his room, so we had the rest of the house to ourselves.

I shrugged. "You're not terrible," I said. "I'm just good at math, the way you're good at swimming."

Jennica was the captain of our school's swim team, even though she was only a junior. She snorted. "Yeah, because swimming is a real life skill," she said. "I'll definitely be able to use that someday."

I knew she was worried about getting into colleges, but I tried to laugh it off. "You never know," I said. "You could have to save a drowning child or something someday."

"Why does it always have be a drowning kid in these

rescue fantasies?" she asked with a smile. "Can't it be a drowning movie star or something?"

"Right," I said. "I can just imagine you pulling Robert Pattinson out of the ocean."

"Or Shia LaBeouf," she said. She paused and giggled. "It could happen."

"You'd probably have to give them mouth-to-mouth," I deadpanned. "You know, to save them, of course."

"You're right. I should definitely go into a career as a celebrity rescue swimmer," Jennica said. She glanced down at the book. "But until then, you'd better teach me about sines and cosines. Just so I have a backup plan if Rob and Shia don't wash up in Plymouth."

I grinned, and for the next forty-five minutes, I slowly went through the equations and formulas we'd talked about in class, and sketched little diagrams to demonstrate everything to her. I was used to this; Jennica always had problems absorbing things in class, and she usually needed some extra explanation, especially in math and science. Her dad, Mr. Arroyo, had been calling me "Miracle Worker Mann" since I helped Jennica bring up a D-plus to a B-minus in seventh-grade earth science.

But I didn't mind at all. I kind of liked my role as her unofficial tutor, especially now, because it gave me some uninterrupted time with her, without Brian nibbling at her neck or trying to slip his arm protectively around her. It felt like it used to feel when it was just the two of us. I wished I could slow down time or freeze the frame so that I could savor it. But like everything good, the moment was fleeting and would be gone before I knew it.

"You got anything to eat?" Jennica asked after she'd successfully completed a problem.

"I'll look." I crossed the kitchen and swung the refrigerator door open. "Not really."

"You must have *something* in there," Jennica protested. "I'm starving."

I frowned at the illuminated shelves. There were a quarter carton of expired milk, five Diet Cokes, three eggs, some carrots, and two slices of pizza left from Saturday night's dinner. Dad used to do the grocery shopping, and after the accident, Mom just forgot sometimes. She worked long hours in Boston, and most nights when she got home, she was too tired to cook.

I'd thought it would get better in July, after the vehicular homicide trial ended. The woman who hit us had been high on drugs. The police couldn't figure out what she was doing in our neighborhood; she lived nine miles away, in North Carver. Mom had gone to the trial every day and had even spoken at the woman's sentencing, but she'd only gotten four years, a suspended license, and a fine. I couldn't believe that was all my dad's life was worth.

I'd hoped that after the sentencing, Mom would have a little bit of closure and would go back to acting somewhat normal. But instead, she'd just started working even more. We hardly ever saw her. She had Pizza Hut, Papa John's, and Fung Wa Chinese in the #1, #2, and #3 spots on speed dial; most of the time, she called from the office to ask me to order food because she wouldn't be home in time for dinner.

I cracked the pizza box and inspected the slices. No

mold growing on them yet. I shrugged and pulled the box out. "How about pizza?" I asked Jennica.

"What kind?"

I checked out the slices more closely. "Pepperoni and sausage, I think."

She wrinkled her nose. "I don't eat meat anymore," she said. "But I guess I could pick it off."

I stared at her. "You don't eat meat anymore?"

"I'm trying to lose weight," she mumbled.

"Since when?" I asked. Jennica had always had curves I was jealous of, and she stayed in great shape, thanks to swimming. I'd had enough Twizzler and Doritos binges at sleepovers with her to know that she'd never been concerned about stuff like that in the past.

She looked down. "I just don't want Brian to think I'm fat."

"Did he say that?"

"No."

I paused, unsure what to say. "So why are you worried?"

She didn't say anything for a long time. Then, in a voice I could barely hear, she said, "I don't know. What if that's why my dad left my mom? Because she got fat?"

"Did your dad say that?" I asked.

She shook her head. "It's just my dad started dating Leanne, like, right away and she's super skinny. And now my mom's put on, like, thirty pounds, and Leanne keeps shrinking. And he's always talking about how beautiful she is."

I took a deep breath. I knew it made me a terrible friend, but I had trouble hearing about Jennica's problems with her mom and dad. I felt bad for her that they had just gotten divorced–they had separated just a month after the accident–but the way Jennica talked about it drove me crazy. It was like her world was ending because her mom and dad no longer lived under the same roof.

But at least they were both alive.

I didn't say that, though. I didn't tell her that her problems paled in comparison to mine. Because that would make me a really horrible friend, wouldn't it? So instead, I pasted on a smile. "I'm sure that had nothing to do with your parents' divorce."

"How do you know?" Jennica asked.

I paused. "I just do," I said. "Besides, that has nothing to do with you and Brian. He's totally in love with you."

Jennica looked down again. "Yeah," she said softly.

I microwaved the pizza for Jennica. After she'd eaten it, dutifully picking off all traces of meat, we did some more sample questions for the trig quiz. She left around five; Logan came traipsing through the front door at six after making out with Sydney in the driveway; and Mom called around seven to say she wouldn't be home for a few hours and to go ahead and eat without her. Like that was anything new.

I ordered fried rice, sweet-and-sour chicken, and beef with broccoli from Fung Wa, and Logan, Tanner, and I ate in silence, none of us making eye contact. After dinner, the boys retreated to their rooms, shutting the doors behind them. I cleaned up the kitchen table, put the leftovers in Tupperware, and loaded the dishwasher. Then I sat down to crack open my fortune cookie.

The one you love is closer than you think, the fortune read. At first I snorted, thinking it meant some guy I loved. And since I didn't love any guy, that was impossible. Then I wondered if it meant something else. I glanced at the ceiling, imagining Logan and Tanner in their rooms, with their stereos on, already entirely separated from the reality of our family. I thought of Mom, forty miles away in Boston and a thousand miles away emotionally.

Finally, I thought of Dad. "The one you love is closer than you think," I said aloud. I looked up and wondered why I didn't believe the words. Well-intentioned adults always told me that my dad was in heaven, watching over me and my mom and brothers. It was an easy thing to say, but if it was true, why couldn't I feel him anymore? Why couldn't I feel anything?

• • •

I had just gotten Tanner to bed, and Logan was locked in his room talking on his cell phone, when Mom walked through the door later that evening. I noticed right away that her eyes were bloodshot.

"What are you doing still up?" she asked, staring at me as she came in through the garage door.

I was sitting in the kitchen, reading *The Great Gatsby* for English class. I liked it way more than I'd expected to, and I'd read past what we were required to read for class this week. I glanced at the clock and realized it was just past eleven. "I guess I lost track of time."

"You really need to get to bed at a reasonable hour,

Lacey, or you're going to be tired for school. We've talked about this before. You can't be irresponsible."

Hearing her say that made my insides twist. Irresponsible was the last thing I was. But I knew the conversation wasn't really about me being up past eleven. "Are you okay?" I asked.

She looked away. "I'm fine," she said. "Is there some dinner left over?"

I hopped up. "I'll make you a plate."

"I don't need–" Mom began, but I cut her off.

"Don't worry, I'll get it," I said. "Just sit down and relax."

She opened her mouth to reply, but nothing came out. Instead, she sank slowly into a seat at the kitchen table, kicked off her heels, and sighed.

"So," I said as I scooped cold fried rice and sweet-and-sour chicken onto a plate, "do you want to talk about it?"

"Talk about what?"

"Whatever's wrong," I said. I slid the plate into the microwave, set it for a minute thirty, and pushed Start. I turned and looked her in the eye. "You've been crying."

"No, I haven't," Mom protested.

"Can you at least not lie to me?" I said. She looked away. "Is it about money?"

"What would make you think that?" she asked. "You know Dad had a life insurance policy and that I'm making plenty. Why do you keep worrying about that?"

I shrugged. "You always seem worried."

She didn't say anything. The microwave beeped. I pulled the plate out and slid it in front of her, along with a fork. I sat down beside her and tried a different tactic. "You were at the office late today."

Mom didn't look at me as she speared a piece of chicken and took a bite. "I had a lot to do," she said after she'd swallowed.

"Like what?"

"I don't want to bore you with it," she said. "Lawyer stuff." She took another bite.

I knew that was code for *Stop asking me questions,* so I changed the subject. "Tanner has to do a diorama for school," I said. "They're supposed to make scale models of their bedrooms. So he'll probably need some supplies."

"Okay," Mom said. "If you e-mail me a list, I'll pick up the materials on my way home from work tomorrow."

"He'll probably need some help with it," I prompted. "I don't think he's done a diorama before."

Mom took another bite and glanced up. "Lacey, I've got a really busy week. My caseload is just unbelievable." She scooped up some rice and added, "Maybe you can help him. You're good at that kind of thing."

"At dioramas?" I couldn't resist asking.

Mom shrugged. "You're more creative than me," she said. "And you have more time. You'd be doing me a big favor, honey. Please?"

"Yeah, okay." I paused and tried to decide how to phrase what I wanted to say. "Look, maybe you could spend some time with Tanner this weekend or something, though. I'm really worried about him."

"Lacey, he's always been quiet. You can't keep worrying about everybody and everything."

"But if I don't," I said before I could think about it, "who will?"

Mom held my gaze. Then she stood up from the table and scraped the remainder of her food into the trash can. She put her plate in the sink and turned to me. "I'm going to go to bed," she said. "You should get some sleep too, honey."

I watched her walk out of the kitchen. She reminded me a little of a ghost. She'd lost a lot of weight since the accident, and now, instead of walking with the purposeful stride of an attorney who knew what she wanted out of life, the way she used to, she seemed to shuffle from place to place, a vacant look on her pale face. I wondered whether she acted like this at her office, too, and if anyone noticed.

I cleaned up the kitchen, rinsed Mom's plate, started the dishwasher, and walked upstairs to my room, wondering how it was possible to have an entire conversation without saying anything at all.

chapter 3

By Wednesday, Sam Stone had gotten his own textbooks, so he didn't have to share with me anymore in trig. And it wasn't like we had any other reason to talk to each other. The rumor was he had moved from somewhere out in western Massachusetts, but I didn't feel like it was my place to ask him why. If anyone knew what it felt like to be drilled with unwelcome questions, it was me.

At lunch that day, I was sitting with Jennica and Brian as usual. He had his right arm draped around her, which I figured must make it tough to eat.

"So that new guy, Sam?" Jennica asked. I looked up,

startled that she seemed to be reading my mind. "You know," she continued, "that guy from our trig class?"

"Yeah," I said.

"So he's hot, huh?" She leaned forward and grinned at me.

"Jennica!" Brian exclaimed, feigning hurt as he pulled her closer.

"Aw, baby, he's not as hot as you," she said.

Brian stuck out his bottom lip in a mock sulk. "Really?"

Jennica giggled. "You're the hottest of the hot." She gave him a quick kiss on the lips.

"No, *you're* the hottest of the hot," Brian said in an equally disgusting voice.

"No, you are," Jennica said, batting her eyelashes.

"No, you are, pookie," Brian said, leaning forward to kiss her.

Pookie?

"I think I just threw up a little in my mouth," I muttered. I stood, and the two of them looked up from their love haze.

"What's wrong?" Jennica asked, blinking at me.

"Nothing. I'm just not hungry anymore. I'll see you later." I grabbed my tray and waited for her to ask me where I was going–after all, there weren't exactly a lot of exciting lunchtime options at Plymouth East–but she had already turned back to Brian.

I threw out my trash and headed out the door to the mostly empty halls. We were allowed to make brief trips to our lockers during lunchtime, but we got in trouble for hanging around too long, so I figured I'd just switch out my morning books for my afternoon ones and go outside. It was overcast, but it hadn't rained yet, and there was a bench under the big oak tree near the senior parking where I sat when I didn't feel like sitting with Romeo and Juliet in the cafeteria.

I had just opened my locker and was digging around in the back, trying to find my compact mirror, when a deep voice coming from the other side of my locker door startled me.

"Hey."

I swung the door closed and found myself face to face with Sam. He was leaning casually against the lockers, his hands jammed in his pockets. I blinked at him, then dropped the English textbook I was holding. It bounced off my backpack and hit me in the calf. I winced.

"Problem?" Sam asked, glancing down at the textbook and then back at me.

"No," I said quickly.

Sam studied me and then smiled, the corners of his mouth creeping slowly upward like a stream of syrup spreading across a pancake. "You sure?" he asked.

"Positive." I felt a little short of breath.

He bent down and picked up my backpack and my textbook in one smooth motion. "Here," he said, handing them to me. "You might need these."

"Thanks." I stared at my feet, willing my face to stop flaming. What was wrong with me? I was reliable, mature Lacey Mann, who could be trusted to behave like a grown-up in any situation. And here I was acting like, well, Sydney.

"So." Sam put his hands back in his pockets. His warm green eyes met mine. "What are you doing out here in the hallway? Shouldn't you be eating with that friend of yours in the cafeteria? Jennica?"

"It's no big deal," I said. "She's with her boyfriend. I just felt like walking around."

"Guess you don't want to watch her and her boyfriend all over each other," he said.

I looked up sharply. "What? No. That's not it."

Sam looked like he didn't believe me. "It would bother me."

I paused. "Okay," I admitted. "Maybe it bothers me a little." I cleared my throat, suddenly desperate to change the subject. "So, um, your old school," I said. "Where is it? I mean, where did you come from?"

"Taunton."

"Oh," I said. "I've been there." It was about thirty minutes away.

"Oh yeah?"

I nodded. "My brother Logan played in a baseball tournament there a few years ago." *Back when he still played baseball,* I added silently. *Back when things were normal.*

"Cool," Sam said. "I used to play ball. Maybe I played against him. Are you a baseball fan?"

"Definitely."

"Sox?" he asked.

I nodded again. "My dad always takes my brothers and

me to Fenway a few times each summer." Then I stopped abruptly, the words caught in my throat as I realized what I'd just said.

"Cool," Sam said, oblivious. "I haven't met a lot of girls who like baseball. Did you guys make it to a lot of games this year?"

I swallowed hard. "No," I said without elaborating.

Sam seemed to register that something was off. He unslouched from the locker and drew himself up to his full height. He was taller than I had realized.

"You okay?" he asked.

"Fine," I said.

"Okay," Sam said uncertainly. He gave me a half smile. "I'll see you in class then, cool?" He turned and walked away.

• • •

The rest of the week sped by, the way the weeks in the fall always did, when your new grade and new classes still felt fresh and exciting. Sam had begun smiling at me in class now and saying hi in the halls like we were friends. I always smiled back and then looked quickly away, as if locking eyes with him would be a dead giveaway that I was beginning to develop a crush.

It's not like it was wrong to feel that way about him. It was just that I figured I didn't have much of a chance. Why bother liking him if the chances of him liking me back as more than a friend were slim to none? Summer

Andrews was already flirting with him, and on Thursday, I saw him sitting at her popular senior table for lunch. I wasn't an outsider–I was on student council and played lacrosse in the spring, and people liked me just fine–but I wasn't a cheerleader either. I was brainy, quiet Lacey who everyone thought of as sweet instead of sexy. And despite what my dad used to tell me freshman year, when I'd come home sometimes on the verge of tears, there wasn't a single guy at Plymouth East who would go for a nice girl over an easy one.

On Saturday morning, I was lying in bed, half-awake, trying to stop thinking about Sam, when the sounds from downstairs snapped my eyes open. I glanced over at the clock: 6:06. Too early for me to be awake. Too early for the TV in the living room to be on. But there was no such thing as too early or too late in our house anymore.

I sat up and listened, wondering what Tanner was watching. It was a pretty safe bet that it was either a cartoon or something to do with animals. He was obsessed with animals. Sure enough, when I went down the stairs a few minutes later and rounded the corner into the dark living room, my little brother was sitting a foot from the TV, his face bathed in the glow from the screen. I could see a giraffe ambling through the wilderness.

"Good morning," I said casually, as if it were normal for him to be sitting there, looking like he wanted to climb inside the TV and escape into the wild himself. Tanner turned his head slightly and nodded before returning his attention to the screen.

I went into the kitchen to make us some breakfast. I was determined to pretend that everything was normal until it actually was.

After scanning the fridge to see if Mom had picked anything up on her way home last night–she had–I turned the stove on and slipped three pieces of wheat toast in the toaster. I pulled out a frying pan, put it on the burner, sprayed it with PAM, and cracked three eggs into it, making sure their edges didn't touch, the way Dad always used to when he made breakfast for us.

A few minutes later, I scooped the eggs, their yolks still runny, out of the pan and onto the toast. When I walked back to the living room, Tanner accepted his plate without even looking up. He was riveted to the screen.

"So what are you watching?" I asked after I'd set two juice glasses down and taken a bite of my toast. I knew it was *The Crocodile Hunter,* one of Tanner's favorite shows, but I wanted him to say it. Ever since the accident, he had retreated further and further into himself, and now he hardly said a word, not even to his friend Jay, who came over to play video games once a week. Although, come to think of it, I hadn't seen Jay for a while now. I wondered if he'd finally given up on Tanner.

Nobody seemed to care but me. I had tried bringing it up with Mom, but she just shrugged and said that it wasn't all that abnormal and that Tanner would deal with things in his own time. But what did she know? She saw her legal assistant ten times more often than she saw her kids; Tanner was usually asleep by the time she got home. I had also tried talking about Tanner with Dr. Schiff, the psychologist my mom made us visit every other Saturday. But she had just told me that it wasn't my responsibility. "You're just a kid," she would always say.

It always made my blood boil.

As usual, Tanner didn't answer my question. Instead, he grabbed the remote and hit the Info button until the name of the show appeared at the bottom of the screen. He shot me a look and returned his attention to the TV.

"This looks like a good one!" I said enthusiastically, as if we were having a normal conversation. I fished for something else to say. "I really like how he explains everything so well. And his accent is really cool. Don't you think?"

Tanner nodded without taking his eyes off the screen. He took another bite of his toast. I pushed mine away. I didn't feel hungry anymore. I made some more cheerful, one-sided small talk before I gave up. Tanner obviously wasn't going to respond. And I had run out of things to say.

"Okay, Tanner," I said, feigning cheerfulness. "I'm going to go hop in the shower."

I had just crossed the living room into the kitchen when I heard Tanner's voice. I stopped and turned around.

"What?" I asked.

He was silent for a minute, and I started to doubt that he'd said anything at all. Maybe I'd imagined it. But then he spoke again.

"You know, he died too," he said clearly, still staring at the TV screen. "The Crocodile Hunter. A stingray got him." He looked at me, evidently expecting some kind of response.

I gulped. "Yeah, I know."

"No one saved him either," he said. Then, he turned the volume up. The conversation was over.

I stood there, my heart thudding in my chest. Guilt and responsibility weighed down on me, squeezing me from the inside out.

A hundred times a day, I thought about how different life would be if I hadn't insisted on taking those extra moments in the bathroom. Or if I had cried out to warn Dad, in that instant before the Suburban hit us. Instead, I hadn't reacted. It had been the only important thing I'd ever had to do in my life, and I'd failed. It was like Tanner said. Nobody saved the Crocodile Hunter.

And I hadn't done anything to save my dad.

• • •

By the beginning of the next week, Sam Stone was the talk of the school. Summer Andrews had apparently decided that he was her big new love interest. It didn't seem to matter to anyone else that Summer actually *had* a boyfriend, Rob Macavey, a senior with big arms, close-cropped dark hair, and eyes that were just a little too close together. Jennica and I agreed that he'd clearly been hit in the head one too many times on the football field.

But Summer, who didn't even have a class with Sam, had decided that she had a crush on him, and so the whole school knew she had called dibs. I couldn't understand why she couldn't just limit the number of guys she tried to pounce on.

In class, Sam and I were apparently friends now. I supposed it was because he didn't know anyone very well yet, and since he sat next to me in two classes, I was a logical person to strike up a conversation with. I was surprised to realize how much I liked talking to him, though. It started to be a routine that he would sit down in trig, grin at me, and rattle off the Red Sox score from the previous night, as well as some kind of commentary about a player who screwed things up—even if the Sox ended up winning. I'd been a Sox fan for years and could practically recite the roster in my sleep, but I'd never known a boy before who would talk to me about sports like I knew what I was talking about. It was nice.

After school on Wednesday, I was surprised to find Sam waiting for me by my locker. I'd had plans to go to the mall with Jennica and then study with her later, but she had texted me after the final bell to say that something had come up with her mom and she couldn't make it. Concerned, I'd texted her back to see what was wrong. Don't worry, she had written. Brian's with me.

"There you are," Sam said as I approached.

"Hey."

"So how's it going?" Sam asked. Was it my imagination, or did he seem nervous?

"Good," I said. I couldn't for the life of me figure out what he wanted.

"So I hear you're really good at trig," he said. "Right?"

I shrugged. "I guess."

"I was just wondering if maybe you could help me study for the test on Monday," he said.

"Yeah, okay." I forced a smile. I was Lacey, the reliable study buddy. I just wasn't sure how he'd figured this out so quickly. "I was going to study with Jennica tomorrow, so you can come over too, if you want."

"Cool, thanks." He paused. "So, do you need a ride home or something?"

"Now?"

"Yeah."

I glanced around. Jennica was gone. I'd probably already missed the bus. And riding with Sam would be preferable to riding with Logan and Sydney any day. "Okay," I said. "That would be great."

I pulled a few books out of my locker and shut it. Sam surprised me by taking my backpack off my arm, slipping my books into it, and tossing it over his shoulder. "C'mon," he said.

I followed him outside. He opened the door of his Jeep for me and tossed our bookbags in the back. I told him how to get to my house, and soon we were cruising down Court Street. The silence between us was beginning to feel stifling.

Finally, I blurted out, "So are you going out with Summer Andrews?" I felt like an idiot the moment the question left my mouth.

Sam looked at me in surprise. "What?"

"Nothing," I mumbled. It wasn't my business.

"Summer Andrews?" he asked after a pause. "That senior girl?"

I nodded.

"What would make you think that?"

"I just heard she liked you."

Sam seemed to consider this for a minute. "She seems nice enough," he said. "But I barely know her."

"I'm sure that'll change."

Sam turned left on Samoset. "She's not really my type."

"Really?" I was baffled. Who was this new breed of boy, immune to Summer's powers? "Oh."

"I like girls who are smart," Sam continued. "You know, girls who don't flirt with every guy in the school. Girls who have a little substance to them. I get the feeling I'm not exactly describing Summer."

"You're right about that," I muttered.

We rode in silence for a few minutes as I tried to process what he'd said. He barely knew me either, but he'd sought me out in the hallway after school. Maybe it *wasn't* just to study.

I was just beginning to feel like maybe I'd gotten it all wrong, when we pulled up in front of my house and Sam turned to me. His eyes looked even brighter than ever, and even when he wasn't smiling, the vague indentations of his dimples remained.

"Listen," he said. He was definitely nervous now. "I was thinking that maybe we could go out sometime. If you want to. I mean, it would be cool to hang out outside of class, you know?"

Was he asking me out? A smile rolled across my face before I could stop it. "That sounds good."

Sam looked like he wanted to say something else. It was so nice, I thought in the silence, to finally have someone look at me for me, not as someone they had to feel sorry for or tiptoe around. Last winter, after the accident, several Plymouth East guys had messaged me on MySpace or stopped me in the halls, and I knew that it was just because I was a minor celebrity for a few weeks. That's when Sydney had first taken an interest in Logan too; it's when we became *somebodies.*

And now, for the first time since the accident, I finally felt like someone was seeing me for something other than that-poor-girl-whose-dad-is-dead. Sam didn't know my history. He didn't know he was supposed to feel sorry for me or whisper about me behind my back or purposely avoid mentioning anything to do with fathers.

And just when I was feeling good, Sam opened his mouth and ruined everything. "I heard about your dad," he said.

I could practically feel the walls coming up around me. The smile fell from my face, and everything went cold. I didn't say anything. I just stared at Sam.

He looked uncomfortable. "Listen, I'm sorry."

"Yeah, well, it's old news." My voice was full of ice.

"If you ever want to talk about it . . . ," Sam said, his voice trailing off.

"Look, I don't need some hero to make it all better, if that's what you're trying to do," I snapped. "I'm *fine.* It happened a long time ago."

"I'm not trying to do that." Sam looked surprised. I could have sworn I saw hurt flicker across his face too, but I didn't care. Who was *he* to be hurt? "I just meant, well, I know how you feel," he added.

I could taste bile in my mouth. I stared at him. Of all

the things people said to me to try to make me feel better, I hated that sentence the most. Sam Stone didn't know how I felt. How could he? I was sick and tired of people who'd had a grandparent die and thought it was the same thing. Or even worse, people who'd had to bury a pet iguana or the dog they'd grown up with. Sure, I felt sad for them, but how could they possibly compare that to losing a parent?

"You have no idea how I feel," I said coldly. I reached into the backseat and grabbed my bookbag. I couldn't get out of the Jeep fast enough.

"But Lacey–"

"Forget it," I said firmly. I fumbled with the door handle and spilled out with my things. I could feel Sam watching me all the way to my front door, but I didn't turn around.

• • •

I was overreacting. I knew it. But I couldn't melt the wall of ice that had formed around my heart in those last few minutes in Sam's Jeep. I hated it when people tried to help me, especially now. Couldn't they see I was dealing just fine? *I* was the person holding my family together. I didn't need anyone's help or pity. Especially not some new guy's. I wondered if he had roved the halls of his old school too, looking for sad girls to save.

So I steadfastly ignored Sam, even when he tried to pass me a note the next morning in trig class, even when he threw a paper airplane at my arm to get my attention. I didn't want to talk to him. He wasn't the person I thought he was; he was nosy, just like the rest of them.

That was what I was thinking about when Brooke Newell arrived in the doorway with a note in her hand. She was one of the seniors who was community college-bound already and was taking an office-assistant class for credit. She handed Mrs. Bost the note, snuck a look around the classroom, waved to Krista Sivrich, and then hurried away.

Mrs. Bost unfolded the note and read it. When she looked up, she stared right at me.

"Miss Mann," she said, "your presence is requested in Mr. Miller's office."

A murmur went through the class, and I swallowed hard. Mr. Miller was the main principal. You didn't get sent to him unless something was really wrong. I certainly hadn't done anything to get myself in trouble, so my first thought was *Mom.* Had something happened to her? Or to Tanner? Could something have happened to Logan since I got out of the car thirty minutes ago?

I stood up and stuffed my notebook and pen into my bag.

"Does it say why he wants to see me?" I asked, hating that my voice sounded nearly as panicked as I felt. Someone in the back of the room snickered, and I heard someone else say, "Ooh, she's in *trouble*!"

"No," Mrs. Bost said. I glanced at Jennica, who looked worried. Then, just because I couldn't help it, I locked eyes with Sam.

"Want me to come with you?" he asked, like it was the

most normal question in the world. I opened my mouth to say no, but Mrs. Bost preempted me.

"I think Lacey is capable of finding the principal's office by herself," she said, giving Sam a look.

Sam glanced at me again and shrugged. I could feel my cheeks getting hot. I strode quickly into the hall before my throat could close up entirely.

chapter 4

Mr. Miller's secretary ushered me into his office right away, which only added to my already heightened sense of panic.

"Is my mom okay?" I asked immediately, without bothering to say hello. "And my brothers?"

"Yes, yes," Mr. Miller said hastily. He looked a little confused. "Of course. As far as I know."

I felt the air I'd been holding in leave my body in a whoosh. "Thank God," I said.

Mr. Miller was silent for a minute, as if waiting for me to say something else. He gestured to a chair facing his desk, and I sat down. He continued to stand, staring down at me. He was tall, well over six feet, and he had a comically thick shock of dark hair—too uniformly brown for a man over the age of fifty—that looked out of place on his egg-shaped head. "He's had hair transplant surgery, for sure," Dad used to murmur to me whenever we'd see Mr. Miller at football games and school concerts.

That's what I was thinking about when Mr. Miller cleared his throat. "Lacey, do you know Kelsi Hamilton?" he asked.

"Yeah," I said. "Her mom has cancer." The moment the words were out of my mouth, I hated myself a little bit for saying them. It was the way everyone identified me: by the sad thing that had happened in my life.

I'd known Kelsi since elementary school, and I'd had a class with her last year, but she was quiet, and we hadn't sat near each other, so we barely ever talked. I knew as well as anyone else in the school that her mom had been diagnosed with lung cancer back in May. Bad news tended to travel fast, whispered near lockers between classes, until everyone was walking around with a piece of your life stuck in their back pocket like a trading card.

"Lacey, Kelsi's mother passed away last Saturday," Mr. Miller said.

"Oh no," I said, my heart sinking for Kelsi. "That's awful."

"Yes," he said, sitting down. He pressed his hands together. "Lacey, I need to ask you a favor. And please, feel free to say no."

"Okay."

"Kelsi is back in school today," he said. "For the first time since her mother, um. . . ."

"Died," I filled in. It was sometimes hard for people to actually say the word. I had gotten used to filling it in, in awkward silences, like I was playing a constant game of Mad Libs with only one word to put in the blanks.

"Yes," Mr. Miller said. "I was wondering whether you might . . . spend some time with her."

"What do you mean?"

Mr. Miller cleared his throat. "Kelsi's father called this morning, and of course she's still very upset. He was hesitant to send her back to school, but apparently she insisted. Now, last year, when your father passed . . ." He paused awkwardly. "Well, I know you had Logan to help you through. At school, anyhow."

I resisted the urge to snort. What exactly had Logan done to help me?

"So I'd like to ask you, as a favor to me–well, to Kelsi, really–if you'd talk to her," Mr. Miller concluded.

"Talk to her?" I echoed.

"You know. Just let her know that you're there for her."

"Oh. Of course," I said right away. After all, Kelsi had to know that I'd understand in a way other people couldn't. I wished I'd had someone like that when my dad died, instead of feeling like such an oddball. Sure, Cody Johnson's dad had died in Iraq when we were all in eighth grade, so I suppose he could identify with me when my dad died. But he never said anything. In fact, I could swear he deliberately avoided me, just like so many other people who didn't know how to act. I wished I could scream at people that I was the same person, that all they had to do was treat me normally. But apparently when you had a parent die, you became some sort of science experiment, to be poked and prodded and stared at.

"I've already spoken with your second-period teachers," Mr. Miller said. "You and Kelsi are both good students, so they have no problem releasing you from class so you can have a chat. Maybe the two of you can take a walk or something."

Well, that sounded supremely dorky. I suspected that Mr. Miller was imagining that when we came back from our stroll, Kelsi wouldn't be upset anymore. I didn't want to be the one to tell him that real life didn't exactly work that way.

"Sure," I said instead.

"Thank you, Lacey." Mr. Miller sighed and looked very relieved, like he had just had a great weight lifted off his slumped shoulders.

I could feel the weight he'd just lifted settle inside my chest. "No problem."

• • •

Back in class, I pretended I didn't notice Jennica's raised eyebrows. I also pretended I didn't see Sam staring at me. Actually, pretty much *everyone* was looking at me. I'm sure they were all wondering what I'd done wrong to be called into the principal's office.

I escaped Jennica's questions after class by mumbling something about Logan being in trouble again. I knew I should have just told her the truth. But I figured that it wasn't my place to be telling people Kelsi's bad news. I knew that the rumor would be all over school in a few hours, but I didn't want to be one of the people to spread it.

Thirty minutes later, I was headed back to Mr. Miller's office with a hall pass, filled with a strange kind of trepidation. I wanted to help Kelsi, but I was almost paralyzed by the fear that I wouldn't know what to say or do. *Relax, Lacey,* I told myself. *You're holding your family together. You can definitely figure out how to help this girl.*

Kelsi was already sitting in Mr. Miller's office when I got there. Her carrot-colored curls, which were usually cute and perky, were hanging limply, like she hadn't thought to wash or comb her hair in days. She looked thin. She was wearing old, faded jeans and a Plymouth East marching band shirt that was too big for her. I stared for a second, realizing this was what I must have looked like in the weeks after the accident, like I didn't care, didn't even realize that people were noticing my disheveled appearance.

"Hey," I said to Kelsi.

Kelsi looked up at me. "Hey," she said. Her eyes looked tired, but not like she'd been crying. Maybe she'd run out of tears. It happened sometimes.

I glanced at Mr. Miller and sat down in the other chair facing his desk. Kelsi was staring at her lap now. She looked like she wanted to disappear. My heart ached a little with the familiarity of it all.

"I'm sorry," I heard myself say after a minute. I hadn't meant to say it. In fact, I hated it when people said that to me. It wasn't like *they* were the ones who had killed my dad. What were they sorry for? But the words escaped before I could stop them.

Kelsi looked up. "Yeah," she said. It seemed like she was having trouble focusing on me.

I glanced at Mr. Miller again. "So," I said, "do you want to take a walk or something?"

The question sounded strange, and I expected Kelsi to react like I was crazy. But instead she just shrugged. "Whatever." Without looking at me, she grabbed her bookbag. "Let's go," she said. I followed her out of the office, thinking for the first time that I might be in over my head.

• • •

Outside the school building, I had to jog to keep pace with Kelsi.

"Wait up," I said. This probably wasn't the bonding experience Mr. Miller had visualized, me speeding after Kelsi while she practically ran to escape me.

By the time we rounded the corner, I realized she was making a beeline for her car, a lime green VW Bug. She slid behind the wheel and slammed the door. I heard the engine turn on, and for half a second, as I stood in front of the car, I half expected her to lay on the gas pedal and run me over. Instead, she just sat there, staring at me. Finally, she rolled down her window. "Well? Are you getting in or what?"

I glanced around. "We could get in trouble," I said. We could get detention for sitting inside our cars during the school day, and suspended for leaving school grounds.

"You really think anyone's going to bust you and me?" Kelsi asked. "The girls with the dead parents?"

She was right. Besides, Kelsi needed me. And my responsibility to help her outweighed the risk. I took a deep breath. "Okay," I agreed.

I opened the car door and slid in. "So. Are we going somewhere?"

Kelsi didn't look at me. "No," she said. "Unless there's somewhere you want to go."

"No," I said quickly.

The car engine continued to hum. The air conditioner was on high, even though it was in the fifties outside.

Just as the silence was getting uncomfortable, I blurted out, "Kelsi, I'm really sorry about your mom."

More silence. I could feel my cheeks flaming. Mr. Miller had obviously picked the wrong person to talk to Kelsi.

Then Kelsi said softly, "Thanks." She glanced at me. "I'm sorry about your dad, too. I never told you that."

"Thank you." I was quiet for a moment. "So are you okay? I mean, how are you?"

Kelsi glanced back out the windshield. She squinted, like the answer to my question might be located on the brick wall of the school. "It's not like it's a big deal or anything," she said finally, still not looking at me. Her words poured out in a rush, like she couldn't wait to get rid of them. "I mean, she'd been sick for a while. We knew it was coming. I should have–I should have been more prepared for it."

I wondered what it was like to have time to say goodbye,

to know the end was coming. Did you have fewer regrets? "But it's not like that makes it any easier," I said.

"But it's supposed to," Kelsi mumbled. "Isn't it?"

She was looking at me like I had all the answers. The truth was, I wasn't even sure what the questions were anymore. "I don't think so," I said finally.

I tried to think of something else to say, the kind of thing I would have wanted someone to say to me. But nothing was coming to me. I sat back in the seat.

"Can you just go away now?" Kelsi asked. "I want to be alone."

I looked at her, surprised. "Um, yeah, sure," I said, hoping she wasn't depressed enough to do something stupid. "Are you sure you're okay?"

She glanced at me. "What do *you* think? Are *you* okay?"

I was taken aback. "Yeah," I said.

She snorted and looked away. "Yeah. You're very convincing."

Her words startled me. I was fine. I was happy. I had gone back to being normal. "I *am* okay," I insisted.

"Whatever," Kelsi said. "But look, I really just want to be alone."

I grabbed my bag and opened the car door. "If you need anything, you can ask me, okay? I mean, I've been through this."

"I know," Kelsi said. She paused and then added, "Thanks." The word was so soft I could barely hear it.

chapter 5

"You have to help me," I told Logan at lunch. As I plunked down beside him in the cafeteria, Sydney looked at me like I'd just arrived from outer space. In Plymouth East terms, maybe I had.

"Hi," Sydney said, glancing around, probably calculating how much my presence at the table was reducing her social status.

"*I* have to help *you*?" Logan said. "With what?"

"With Kelsi Hamilton," I said.

"Oh yeah, I heard her mom died," Logan said casually, like it was no big deal. "Bummer."

"It's all over school," Sydney chipped in. "Did you only just hear about it? I've known since, like, nine this morning."

"Now it's a contest?" I asked. I refrained from adding that I'd known earlier than that.

Sydney mumbled something and made a face. I turned back to Logan. "Yeah, Lo, her mom died. It's horrible."

He shrugged. "I guess. I mean, it's not like we really know her."

"*I* know her," I said.

Logan raised an eyebrow. "Since when?"

"Since . . . always," I said. I didn't think what had happened this morning was any of his business. But I let myself gloat, just a little bit, that Mr. Miller had asked for my help, not his.

"Okay," Logan said. "But what does that have to do with me?"

I took a deep breath and began to explain the idea I'd been thinking about since I'd gotten out of Kelsi's car two hours ago. "It has everything to do with you. I thought maybe one day this week we could get Cody Johnson and the three of us could get together with Kelsi after school."

Logan and Sydney stared at me like I'd suggested that we eat worms. "Why would we do that?" Logan asked.

"To show her that she's not alone."

Logan rolled his eyes, and exchanged looks with Sydney. "Lacey," he said slowly, like he was talking to a child, "just because our dad died doesn't mean you have to fix everyone else who loses a parent."

I stared back. "I'm not doing that. Maybe I just want to help. What's wrong with that?"

Logan shook his head. I was surprised to see anger in his eyes. "You know, Lacey, maybe for once you could just let things go, you know? Can't you just grow up and move on?"

"What are you talking about?" I demanded, suddenly aware that my voice had risen an octave.

"You know exactly what I'm talking about."

I stood up abruptly. "You know, Logan, I'm just asking for a little help," I said. "But if you can't do that, forget I ever said anything."

• • •

I was still simmering when Jennica met me at my locker after school. "We still on for studying today?" she asked.

"Of course," I said. "Why wouldn't we be?"

She cleared her throat. "I don't know. I heard about Kelsi. I thought maybe you had to go talk to her or something. Is that why Mr. Miller called you in this morning?"

I averted my eyes.

"How come you couldn't tell me that when I asked you?" she said. There was accusation in her voice.

"I don't know," I said. "I guess I didn't feel like it was my business to talk about it."

"But I'm your best friend." She paused. "Is it because you think I wouldn't understand?"

"No," I said too quickly. "Of course not."

"You know, Lacey, having someone die isn't the only way to lose a parent."

I just looked at her. *Not again,* said the voice in my head.

"It was hard for me when my parents got divorced," she went on. "But you act like it's no big deal, just because my dad is still alive."

I bit my tongue. Hard. I didn't want to get into this with her. I knew it bothered Jennica that I didn't ask her about her parents' divorce very often. And it wasn't that I didn't care. It was just that I couldn't compare a divorce to a death. She could tell her dad she loved him any time she decided to. My chances, on the other hand, were all gone. Forever.

"I'm sorry," I said finally.

Jennica sighed. "I know."

I was just about to say something else when I saw Sam approaching. I began shoving books from my locker into my bag. Jennica furrowed her brow. "What's wrong with you?"

"Nothing," I said, just as Sam walked up. Jennica looked at him, then at me, and stepped back.

"Hey," he said. He smiled at me. "So, are you two still studying this afternoon?"

I shrugged.

"Can I still study with you?" Sam tried again.

I took a deep breath. I didn't want to care. But I did. "I don't think that's a good idea."

"I don't even know what I said to make you upset," Sam said. He was standing so close that I could feel his breath on my hair. It gave me goose bumps. "Look, can I talk to you for a minute? There's something I really need to tell you."

I looked away. "Maybe later," I said, trying to sound

casual. "Jennica and I are in a rush now. We've got to catch a ride with my brother and his girlfriend before they leave without us."

I slammed my locker door shut, grabbed Jennica's arm, and walked away before Sam could say anything else.

• • •

Jennica waited to bring Sam up until we were sitting at my kitchen table forty-five minutes later with two Diet Cokes, a bag of microwave popcorn, some Twizzlers Jennica had brought, and our trig books open in front of us.

"So, are you going to explain what that was all about?" she asked.

I fiddled with the edge of the popcorn bag and then popped a few pieces in my mouth. "It's nothing."

Jennica chomped on a piece of licorice. "Try again."

I sighed. "Fine. He drove me home yesterday, and I actually thought for, like, a minute that maybe he liked me. Then he said he'd heard about my dad and that he knew how I felt." I made a face.

"Okay," Jennica said, waiting for me to go on. "And?"

I shrugged. "That's it."

"Let me get this straight," she said. "The hot new guy, who every girl at school–including Summer Andrews–is into, offers you a ride, has clearly been asking around about you, and says something thoughtful. And this is a problem *why*?"

"Jennica, there's a difference between liking someone

and feeling sorry for them," I said. "Don't you understand that? The last thing I need is some guy's pity."

"Okay," Jennica said slowly. "Only, what if he doesn't pity you? What if he's just trying to be nice? Because he likes you?"

"Well, I don't need someone telling me he knows how I feel," I grumbled. "You know how much I hate that."

"Yeah, well, sometimes you don't give people a chance," Jennica said.

I resisted the urge to snap at her that the only person she gave a chance to anymore was her boyfriend. I didn't want to sound jealous. "Jennica," I began. I paused, unsure of what I wanted to say. I wanted to tell her that I missed her, that I missed this, that I missed *us.* I wanted to tell her that there was a huge gulf between us, and I didn't know how to cross it anymore. But before I had a chance to say anything, the doorbell rang.

I swung the door open to find Jay Cash, Tanner's friend from down the street, standing there. "Hi, Jay," I said, surprised to see him. His visits had been getting less and less frequent.

"Hey," he said. He had hit a growth spurt over the summer, but he still had the same goofy grin and wore the faded, dingy Red Sox cap he'd been wearing every day for the past three years. He was holding a baseball glove. "Is Tanner home? I was wondering if he wanted to play catch or something."

"Yeah, hang on," I said. "He's in his room."

"My mom sent me down," Jay added, shifting his

weight uneasily from one foot to the other. He looked a little guilty. *That explains it,* I thought.

I invited Jay in and went upstairs to get my brother. I knocked, and when there was no reply, I pushed the door open.

Tanner was squatting in the corner of his room near the window, peering into the cage where his hamster, McGee, lived. Dad had always talked about letting us get a dog, but we'd never gotten around to it. After the accident, Tanner, who had vowed he'd become a vet one day to help save all the sick animals he could, had begged for a puppy. Mom had been firm on saying no; she said we had enough to worry about. But as Tanner's silence deepened, she finally broke down and agreed to get him a hamster, as long as it stayed in his room. He'd had McGee, a chubby puff of brown and white fur, since May.

"Hey, Tanner," I said as I walked in. "Jay's here. He wants you to come out and play catch with him."

Tanner was silent for a minute. "Why?"

"Because you're friends," I said gently. "Right?"

Tanner glanced back at McGee, who was curled up in the corner of his cage, his little hamster chest rising and falling in sleep. "I'm busy."

"Tanner," I said, "you're not really that busy. McGee's just sleeping. Why don't you go play with Jay for a while? You guys haven't hung out in ages."

Tanner shrugged.

"Don't you hang out with him at school?"

Tanner shook his head.

"Why?" I asked. "Have you made other friends?" These

were the questions a parent should be asking, I knew. But Mom didn't seem to know how to talk to us anymore.

"Why not?" I asked when he shook his head.

No reply.

"Is it because you feel sad? About Dad?"

He shook his head.

"Because the other kids at school tease you?" I tried again.

More head shaking.

"Because you feel left out when people talk about their dads?" I guessed again. I didn't know what else to say. "Buddy," I said finally, "I think you should go outside with Jay. Just for a little while." I paused, trying to think of what Dad would do. But then again, Tanner had never had this problem when Dad was around. Maybe Dad wouldn't understand it any better than I did. "You can come home whenever you want to," I said.

To my surprise, Tanner slowly stood up. "Okay," he said. He grabbed his baseball glove off the corner of his bookshelf.

My heart lurched a little. I put my hand on his shoulder as we walked out of the room and started down the stairs. "Good," I said. "It'll be fun."

Tanner stopped and looked up at me. "It's not fair," he said.

"What's not fair?"

"I'm not supposed to have fun," he said after a long pause. "Dad doesn't get to." He was gone before I had a chance to open my mouth.

chapter 6

The whole next week, I avoided Sam's eyes, ignored his notes in class, and tried not to feel guilty when I noticed the C+ on his trig test. I knew that if I'd helped him study, he could have gotten a higher grade. But I couldn't take care of everyone. And there was someone far more important to pay attention to: Kelsi Hamilton. Knowing that I was the only one who knew how she felt *and* cared about helping her weighed on me. I watched her walk through the hallways like a zombie, floating from one class to the next.

The whispers were what bothered me the most.

"Did you hear about Kelsi?" was the most common

refrain. Some people didn't even bother to whisper. But the worst, by far, were the students who tried to capitalize on her grief to win extra popularity points. People who wouldn't have given her a second look before her tragedy now wanted to be all buddy-buddy with her so that they could be at the center of attention when anyone asked about her.

"Why can't people just be normal to Kelsi?" I exploded to Jennica in the cafeteria on Thursday. A hush had fallen over the room as Kelsi walked in. Dozens of pairs of eyes followed her as she sat down at a table by herself and pulled a brown bag out of her backpack without looking up. "We should invite her to sit with us," I added.

Jennica looked at me. "Then you're just acting like everyone else, aren't you?" she asked. "Trying to get a piece of her?"

I glared. Jennica knew very well that wasn't what I was doing. But she was grumpy today because Brian was home sick. Jennica had already asked several times whether I thought she should skip school and bring him chicken noodle soup. I had responded that I thought he was capable of opening a can of Campbell's on his own. She just gave me a look and began mumbling about how when you really loved someone, you shared everything, even germs.

Personally, I thought that was kind of gross.

"I'm not trying to get a piece of her," I said through gritted teeth. Jennica shrugged and took a bite of her tofu sandwich on whole wheat. She was still on her weight-loss kick, but I saw her staring lustily at the fries on my tray each day while she munched on carrot sticks.

Just then, I noticed two of my least favorite people in the school, Tali Bonner and Tatiana Roseberg, approaching Kelsi's table, their matching raven-colored hair swinging behind them like pendulums. I stiffened. Tali and Tatiana, known collectively as the TaTas–and not just because of the first letters of their names–were senior cheerleaders and two of the most popular girls at Plymouth East, right beneath Summer on the social scale. Tatiana's romantic exploits with underclassmen were legendary, while Tali was rumored to only go for college guys.

Of course, they were also the worst when it came to situations that might increase their popularity. In fact, it was because of them that I'd first realized that I was no longer just plain old Lacey Mann. I was Lacey Whose Dad Died. I had been eating in the cafeteria with Jennica on my third day back to school when they had sauntered up, arm in arm, smiling at me.

"Oh my God, you must be so depressed!" Tali had started off without even a hello.

"*So* depressed," Tatiana had chimed in. I looked around to make sure they were actually talking to me. They confirmed it by settling into two of the empty seats at our table.

"I mean, you must feel *so* guilty," Tali had continued in the same tone of voice you'd use to compliment someone's outfit.

I just looked at her. Fortunately, Tatiana jumped in to explain. "Because you were with your dad in the car," she said.

"And you didn't save him," Tali added helpfully, a big smile plastered across her heavily made-up face.

Suddenly, the tears that I'd been holding back so successfully were running down my face in rivers. Tatiana looked disgusted; Tali looked delighted. As I jumped up from the table, it felt like the whole cafeteria was watching me.

It was the last time I'd cried. Since then, the tears wouldn't come.

The TaTas never spoke to me or acknowledged me again, but I'd heard them telling people that their *friend* Lacey was still *really* depressed, and they were doing everything they could to help, because they cared so much. More than once, I'd heard people ask them how I was doing–instead of asking me. The whole thing had made my blood boil.

And now they were zeroing in on Kelsi.

"I gotta go," I said to Jennica. I jumped up, dropped my trash in the garbage, and slid into an empty seat at Kelsi's table just as the TaTas were getting started.

I hadn't heard the opening of their conversation, but Kelsi was staring blankly at them. I wasn't sure if it was the blankness of someone who couldn't understand why two of the most popular cheerleaders in school were standing at her table, or the blankness of someone who didn't care about anything anymore, because nothing else mattered when one of your parents had just died.

"Hi, Kelsi!" I chirped in my brightest voice, forcing a megawatt smile that could trump any cheerleader's. The

TaTas turned to me, matching blank expressions on their faces.

Kelsi looked at me. Her eyes were bleary. "Hi?" she said. The TaTas were still staring at me, but their blankness had turned to annoyance.

"Kelsi, did you forget?" I bubbled, making it up as I went. "You told me you'd help me with my history homework. I'm so nervous about the test I have today."

"Homework?" she repeated.

"Yeah, you know, the assignment you promised to help me with? But I, uh, get distracted with people around. No offense." I smiled fakely at the TaTas. "Let's go outside so I can concentrate."

Kelsi glanced at the TaTas. "Yeah, okay."

"What was that all about?" Kelsi asked as we walked outside.

"Didn't you see the way they were looking at you?" I asked, incredulous. "It was like you were some kind of prize."

Kelsi shrugged. "I didn't notice."

We were walking toward the parking lot now, and I wondered if we were going to have another bizarre rap session in Kelsi's car.

Suddenly, Kelsi pulled a pack of cigarettes from her backpack and shook the box a little until one fell out. I watched, wide-eyed, as she lit up as if she'd done it a thousand times before.

"You *smoke*?" I asked, so surprised that I actually stopped in my tracks.

Kelsi took a long drag on the cigarette and then

exhaled, the smoke forming a lingering cloud as it exited her mouth. "So?"

I paused. "But your mom died of *lung cancer.*"

The words hung in the air between us, big and ugly.

When Kelsi finally spoke, she didn't look at me, but there was something in her voice that hadn't been there before.

"The doctors lie," she said. The words were clipped, cold, and filled with something ugly that felt familiar to me.

"What do you mean?"

Kelsi stared out toward the parking lot. "My mom never smoked a cigarette in her life. So how does a person who hasn't smoked, and has hardly ever been around smokers, die of lung cancer?"

I looked at her, surprised. "She never smoked?"

"No." She took another drag off her cigarette. "So what's the point anyhow? I mean, if you can do everything right and then still die of lung cancer, why bother?"

I wanted to tell her not to smoke, that it was bad for her, and stupid, too, but this hardly seemed like the time.

"And you know what the best part is?" Kelsi continued. "It could be hereditary. So yeah, there's a higher chance that I'll get it, because my mom had it. So what the hell?"

"Yeah, but smoking doesn't seem like the answer," I said. I eyed her cigarette warily, trying to understand her mixed-up feelings. It was probably a little similar to having a dad who always buckled up and always drove the speed limit and then got killed in a car accident that never should have happened. "Life just isn't fair sometimes," I added, more to myself than to her.

"Yeah, thanks for telling me," she said sarcastically. "I hadn't noticed." She dropped her cigarette on the ground and stubbed it out with the toe of her sneaker. "So," she said, "you wanna skip or what?"

I stared at her. "You mean, like, now?"

Kelsi rolled her eyes. "You can't be perfect *all* the time," she said. "Besides, do you really think we're going to get in trouble? Seriously. We're the kids all the teachers feel sorry for."

Kelsi had a point. All those teachers who had buzzed around me with fake, cheerful smiles, telling me that they wanted to help if there was anything they could do, would probably look the other way if I was caught, wouldn't they?

"Okay," I said after a minute. I took a deep breath and tried to tell myself this was something I had to do to help Kelsi. "Let's go."

And for the first time that week, a small smile appeared on Kelsi's face.

chapter 7

As we pulled out of the school lot, Kelsi fiddled with the radio distractedly. It made me a little nervous that she wasn't paying enough attention. Then again, I always felt uneasy in cars since the accident.

Once we'd driven for a few minutes, she rolled the windows down and turned the stereo up. The new Star Beck song was on. The wind whipped through my hair, getting colder as Kelsi picked up speed. We were approaching the interstate, and I wondered if we were going to get on. Cape Cod was just to the south, over the Bourne Bridge. If we headed north, we'd be in Boston in under an hour, and honestly, my mom would probably kill me if she found out.

"Where are we going?" I finally shouted over the wind and music.

Kelsi didn't answer, and I wasn't sure she had heard me. Then she said, "I don't know. Does it matter?"

I shrugged. The on-ramp for the interstate was coming up, but Kelsi zoomed right past it, shooting toward Milton Park, where my mom used to take me and Logan to play when we were kids. Kelsi pulled in, but instead of parking, she looped slowly around in the lot and headed back the way we came.

We drove a few minutes more in silence until we were back on Summer Street. I wasn't paying attention until Kelsi suddenly slowed and made a hard right into a parking lot I'd managed to avoid all year.

I froze in my seat. "What are we doing here?" I asked, all my nerves on edge. I hoped that she was just turning around, like she had at Milton Park. But instead, she pulled neatly into a parking space in the nearly deserted lot.

She cut the ignition and climbed out of the car, pulling her cigarettes out of her pocket.

I stayed in the car, glued to my seat. My limbs felt stiff and uncooperative, but I wasn't sure what I wanted them to do anyhow.

We were at St. Joseph's Cemetery, a place I hadn't set foot in since my dad's funeral. It was a pretty place, really, with lots of rolling green hills and chirping birds and squirrels running around like nothing was wrong. Sunlight trickled down beautifully in little patches through the leaves of the lush, overgrown oak trees that dotted the property. But it was impossible to see it as a nice, peaceful place. I hadn't wanted to see it at all, in fact, and deliberately turned away every time I passed it.

My mom went every Sunday morning to lay flowers on Dad's gravestone. Sometimes, early on, Logan had gone with her, although now he was usually too busy with Sydney. Tanner went occasionally too.

But I always refused. Seeing Dad's grave made it real. I wasn't delusional; I knew he was dead. But sometimes I could still wake up in the morning, and for those foggy few seconds before reality dawned, I'd have a fleeting instant of wondering what Dad was going to make for breakfast.

I loved those moments. And I had the feeling that there would be fewer of them–or that they would disappear entirely–if I started visiting his grave. I didn't want to remember him as a cold piece of stone or an eight-by-four patch of green grass.

I took a deep breath and scrambled out of the car. "I don't want to be here," I announced, walking over to Kelsi, who was fiddling with her pack of cigarettes.

She leaned back against her car door and drew in a deep breath of smoke, which she exhaled suddenly with a sharp cough, leading me to wonder if she was really the experienced smoker she seemed to want me to think she was.

"You want one?" she offered, holding the pack out.

"I don't smoke."

Kelsi rolled her eyes. "Neither did I," she said. "Things change."

We stood there in silence for a minute. I was trying

very hard to forget where we were. I felt cold inside. I swallowed hard a few times, a weird pang in my chest.

"Give me one," I blurted out, surprising myself with the desperation in my voice. Kelsi looked at me with mild interest, then handed me the pack of cigarettes.

"You have to shake it," she said, smiling at my hesitation, "to get one out."

I nodded, feeling silly, and did as she said until a cigarette dropped into my hand. I had never smoked before. I'd had it drilled into me from an early age that smoking would kill you. But then again, so would driving in your own neighborhood on a Saturday morning with your kids.

I tentatively put the cigarette between my lips and Kelsi took a step closer. She flicked the lighter a few times until it lit and held it to the tip of my cigarette. "Inhale," she commanded.

I did, watching as the cigarette ignited with the force of my breath. All of a sudden, my lungs filled with smoke–sharp, dark, itchy smoke–and I began to cough, hard at first and then even harder, unable to control myself. I dropped the cigarette and Kelsi quickly stubbed it out while I doubled over, coughing some more. It felt like I couldn't get the smoke out of my lungs. I gasped for air.

Kelsi shook her head. "You suck at this."

I coughed some more and glared at her. "Shut up."

Kelsi watched me hacking up my lungs, and to my surprise, she started to giggle, slowly at first and then harder.

I looked down at my stubbed-out cigarette and lifted a

hand to my cheek, which I knew was red from all the coughing. In a dark, weird way, I had to admit, it was a funny scenario.

Kelsi's laughter was contagious, and soon, I was giggling and then laughing too. Here we were, two Goody Two-shoes, smoking in the cemetery parking lot during school hours. The Plymouth East gossip mill would never have believed it.

In that moment, I felt closer to Kelsi than I had to anyone–even Logan or Jennica or my mom–in ten months. After all, Kelsi knew exactly how I felt, in a way that few people did.

It was also the first time I could remember laughing–*really* laughing–in a long time. I had to admit, it felt good.

Then, I realized that the sound of Kelsi's laughter had changed. The giggles were coming in gasps, and they trembled on their way out.

She was crying. Hard. Tears were rolling down her cheeks. I had never seen anyone laugh and sob hysterically at the exact same time. I knew I was supposed to do something, but I didn't know what.

"Kelsi?" I asked tentatively. I watched, feeling totally helpless, as she leaned back hard against her car and slid slowly down it, eventually collapsing to the ground, a puddle of limp limbs, still crying. The laughter was gone now, having given way to pure sobs that racked her whole body. My heart ached.

Slowly, uncomfortably, I knelt down, intending to pull her into a hug, because it was all I could think to do. But when my fingertips touched her upper arm, she jerked angrily away, as if I had burned her with the tip of one of her cigarettes.

"Leave me alone!" she barked. "Just go away!"

She drew her knees up to her chest and put her face down on them, working herself into a little ball. I didn't know what to do, so I sat down beside her, feeling miserable.

Eventually, Kelsi's sobbing slowed. I tentatively put my hand on her arm again, and when she didn't shake me off, I slipped it loosely around her back in a sort of half-hug, the best I could manage side by side on the ground. We sat like that for a while as Kelsi wiped at her eyes.

"It gets better," I said.

Kelsi shook my hand off her shoulders. "Oh yeah? When?"

I didn't have an answer. *Did* it get better? Sure, I wasn't the crying mess that I was for the first few weeks after Dad's death. I was fine now. I never cried anymore. But there was still an emptiness inside me that wouldn't go away. And sometimes, I was sure that the empty space was growing bigger and bigger, threatening to swallow me whole.

"So, do you want to go see your mom's grave or something?" I asked.

"No," she snapped.

"Oh," I said, caught off guard and not sure what else to say.

Kelsi sighed. "I just want to go home," she said finally,

in a voice so quiet I could barely hear her. "I just want to go back to the way it was before."

I knew exactly what she meant. And she knew I knew.

Silently, we stood up, dusted our jeans off, and got back into the car. As Kelsi started the engine and pulled out of her spot, I looked out the window, turning my face away from the rolling green cheerfulness of the darkest place I'd ever seen. I knew that as we pulled back on to Summer Street, if I looked toward the cemetery, I would see my father's grave. It was on the crest of a little hill midway into the cemetery. Although I'd only been there once, the day of his funeral, his grave's location was burned into my mind, and I knew it as well as I knew the location of my own fingers and toes.

• • •

It was nearly three-thirty by the time we turned onto Main Street on our way back to school. We were just a few blocks inland from the harbor, the same rocky, jagged jut of coastline the Pilgrims had landed on four hundred years ago. I could smell the salt in the air and feel it on my skin, the way I always could when the wind was blowing west. Today, even though the afternoon had warmed up, the breeze made me shiver.

Kelsi and I weren't talking, but it wasn't the same kind of weird, uncomfortable silence that had filled the car during our roundabout drive to the cemetery. Something had shifted between us.

"Hey, Kelsi?" I said as we pulled up to a red light.

She looked at me, a question on her face.

"What if we did this more often?" I ventured.

Kelsi laughed. "Skip school so we can go smoke and cry in the parking lot of the cemetery?"

"No." I smiled. "*This.* I mean, it feels normal now, doesn't it? I mean, not *normal* normal. But more normal than we feel at school, anyhow. What if we got together sometimes?"

The light changed, and Kelsi eased her foot back onto the gas. She gave me a funny look. "Why would we do that? It's not like we're even friends."

Ouch, I thought. But still, I pressed on. "Because with me, you don't have to be Kelsi Whose Mom Died. And I don't have to be Lacey Whose Dad Died. You know?"

Kelsi was silent for so long that I began to think she wasn't going to respond. Then, finally, in an almost inaudible voice, she said, "Yeah. I know."

"Maybe we can see if Logan wants to come too," I said. As Kelsi turned left into the school parking lot, kids were pouring out of the buildings toward the cars. The final bell must have just rung.

"Whatever," she said casually, like she didn't care. But then she added, "Maybe we should ask Mindy Rodriguez, too. She's a freshman. I heard her mom died last year."

"And Cody Johnson," I said.

Kelsi frowned. "So you want to start, like, some kind of club for kids with dead parents or something?"

"Not really." The plan was forming in my mind as I spoke, and I wasn't sure if it was stupid or not. "What if it's just us getting together and hanging out sometimes without feeling like outcasts?" I asked. "I mean, we can talk about our parents if we want to. But we don't have to. We can feel like we did before."

Kelsi pulled into a parking spot, cut the ignition, and stared at her lap for a long time. Finally, she looked up at me. "Okay," she said. "I'm in."

chapter 8

Once I'd had the idea of getting us all together, I couldn't stop thinking about it. I thought about it at school. I thought about it at home. I lay in bed at night thinking about how I just might be able to help everyone who hurt the same way I did. I imagined scenarios in which the program was such a success, I would be asked to travel all around the country to talk to grown-ups about how to help kids who'd lost a parent.

But I was getting ahead of myself. I hadn't talked to anyone but Kelsi about it, and I hadn't even researched how to go about setting up an informal group of teens who got together to be with other people who didn't make them feel like outcasts. Still, I knew in my gut that it was something I had to do. I just had to figure out how.

Jennica came over after school on Friday to do our weekend trig homework, and then my mom drove us to Jennica's house. I'd told her we were having a sleepover, which wasn't exactly a lie, since I really was sleeping over at Jennica's place. But we were also going to a party at Brooke Newell's house, and I knew my mom would probably say no if I asked her. Ever since the accident, she'd been completely freaked out about anything that involved teenagers, cars, and possibly alcohol. Not that I blamed her. But it wasn't like we were going to drink and drive. I knew what could happen when you got in a car, even when alcohol wasn't a factor.

"It'll just be me and Tanner tonight at home," my mom said as she drove. She glanced in the rearview mirror at Tanner, who was sitting beside Jennica and gazing out the window.

"Why?" I asked. "Where's Logan going?"

"Over to Will's house to play some video game, I think," Mom said absently. "Or maybe to watch movies. He's having a sleepover too, like you girls."

Jennica and I exchanged looks. Will was Logan's friend last year, but they hardly ever talked anymore, thanks to the fact that Logan now spent all his time with Sydney. I doubted he was spending Friday night at Will's, but Will was the excuse he used most weekends to sneak out of the house. I hadn't blown his cover yet, although with the way he acted toward me sometimes, it was pretty tempting.

I wondered if Logan would be at Brooke's party too. I'd always assumed that the Will lie was a cover for sneaking out with Sydney. But maybe my brother was going to more of these popular-crowd parties than I realized.

My mom dropped us at Jennica's, and after kissing me absently on the cheek, she drove away, back to the silent bubble of our house.

"She's really out of it, isn't she?" Jennica said quietly.

I sighed. "It's been like that for a while."

Jennica nodded. "Come on," she said as she started toward the door. "We don't have much time to get you dressed. I told Brian we'd pick him up in an hour."

I looked down at what I was wearing: my favorite pair of jeans, flip-flops, a pale pink tee, and a gray hoodie that I'd gotten at the Star Beck concert Jennica and I had gone to a year and a half ago in Boston. It had the redheaded singer's face emblazoned on the back and a handful of little sequined stars down the right front side. It was one of my favorite pieces of clothing, and I figured the sequins dressed it up enough to make it party appropriate. "What's wrong with what I have on?" I asked.

Jennica rolled her eyes. "Everything," she said.

She led me inside, past the kitchen, where the fridge door was open, obscuring all but the feet of Jennica's mom, who was standing behind it, looking inside.

"Hi, girls!" she said, straightening up with a smile. "I was just about to throw something in for dinner. Hungry?"

She shut the refrigerator door, and I couldn't help staring. I'd known Mrs. Arroyo for years now, and she'd always been the quintessential mom, so much so that I'd caught myself feeling jealous lots of times this year when my mom had retreated inside herself so much. I was used to seeing Mrs. Arroyo in jeans and a T-shirt, or covered up in an apron, with her hair tied back and little makeup on.

But today, she was wearing a denim miniskirt and a halter top. Her hair was loose and had been curled at the ends, and she had on way too much blush and lipstick.

Jennica audibly sighed. "We'll be in my room, Mom," she said. Then, before I could say anything or react, she grabbed my hand and dragged me toward the staircase. She smiled an obviously fake smile at me. "Divorce is fun!" she said brightly.

It had been ages since I'd been to Jennica's house. She was always busy with Brian, and I supposed I'd been glad to have the distance between us; seeing her perfect family depressed me. But is this what had happened to all of them since I'd stopped paying attention?

I followed Jennica upstairs. She pulled me into her room and shut the door behind us, then she flopped onto her bed.

"What's the deal with your mom?" I asked, sitting down beside her.

"She thinks she's a teenager. Apparently, it's her plan to get her 'sexy' back." Jennica shrugged. "I mean, good for her, I guess. But *I* would never dress like that."

"Me neither," I said with a shudder. "And my mom would kill me if I did."

Jennica snorted. "Don't be so sure," she said. "Your mom looks about as tuned in as mine does."

I was silent. She was right.

Jennica shook her head and got up from the bed. "Anyhow," she said. "Let's get you dressed."

For the next twenty minutes, I felt like a Barbie doll as Jennica made me try on outfit after outfit. She had determined that we should both be wearing tight jeans and cleavage-baring tops tonight, like all the popular girls.

"Okay," I said slowly. "That sounds good. But I have two problems."

Jennica simply raised an eyebrow and waited for me to go on.

"First, it's like forty degrees outside," I said. "I think it's past the skimpy-top-wearing season."

Jennica rolled her eyes. "Fine, so we'll wear skimpy tops with jackets. Happy?"

I smiled at her without answering. "However, the second, and much more pressing, issue is that I *have* no cleavage. So a cleavage-baring top is pretty much impossible."

"Girl!" Jennica said, shaking her head. "Don't you know how to work what you have?"

What I *had* was an A-cup. But in Jennica's frighteningly capable hands, and with the help of pads from an old bra she'd grown out of a couple years ago and some double-sided tape, I suddenly looked a lot different than usual in a pair of long black pants, high heels, and a low-cut sparkly silver tank top of Jennica's that made me look much curvier than I really was.

"Voilà!" she exclaimed, stepping back to admire her admittedly impressive handiwork. I just stared at myself in the mirror.

"How'd you do that?" I asked in astonishment.

"I'm not done yet," Jennica said. It took her ten more minutes to apply bronzer, blush, lipstick, eyeliner, and mascara to my usually bare face. I looked in the mirror with trepidation, expecting to see something horrific (or at least something like her over-blushed mom). Instead, I looked . . . good.

"Hellooooo, hot mama!" Jennica said, grinning at me in the mirror.

I giggled. "This is . . . different. You're like a miracle worker!"

Jennica shrugged. "Nah," she said. "I didn't do anything. I just played up what you've already got!"

I stared at the mirror and shook my head in amazement. She was right; I did look like me. Just a prettier version.

• • •

Ten minutes later, Jennica had changed too–into jeans, heels, and a sparkly purple tank (the difference being that she actually had real curves to fill it out)–and I had persuaded her that I needed a cardigan so I wouldn't freeze to death. Grudgingly, she had handed one over. I intended to bring my Star Beck hoodie, too, because I figured it would be cold enough outside that I'd want to layer up.

We walked downstairs and found Jennica's scantily clad mom removing a pizza from the oven while Jennica's little sister, Anne, sat at the table, drinking a glass of milk.

"Just in time for dinner, girls!" Mrs. Arroyo exclaimed. Jennica started to protest, but her mom turned firm. "Jennica! I can't send you and Lacey out of here with empty stomachs, now can I?" Without waiting for an answer, she added, "Wash some salad mix and get the dressing out, will you? Lacey, what would you like to drink?"

I sat next to Anne and flashed her a smile. She looked up from her glass, and I tried not to giggle when I noticed her milk mustache.

"Hey, you," I said. "How's it going?"

"Fine," she answered gruffly. "What's up with you?" Anne was twelve and right in the middle of that tough phase when *you* know you're grown up, but the rest of the world still treats you like a kid. I knew she was trying to sound as adult as possible. I played along.

"Not much," I said with a shrug.

"Got a boyfriend?" she asked, turning her gaze back to her milk.

I looked at her, surprised. "Um, no," I said. "Do you?"

She glanced at Jennica, who was pouring salad into a bowl. Then she returned her attention to me. "Yeah," she said casually, "I got a few options."

I looked over at Jennica in time to see her roll her eyes. It had always bugged her that Anne seemed to copy every move she made. Her younger sister had insisted she was "playing the field" when Jennica was single, but now that Jennica had Brian, Anne was always saying cryptic things about how she had lots of boyfriend options.

"Having a boyfriend isn't all it's cracked up to be, kiddo," Jennica muttered. I turned and glanced at her, wondering what that was all about.

We scarfed down our pizza and salad in the same kind of silence that pervaded my house. This surprised me. I'd just assumed that Jennica's family was just as it had always been.

Apparently, I was wrong.

After Jennica and I had put our plates in the sink and wrapped the remaining slices of pizza in foil, Mrs. Arroyo stood up to give Jennica a hug and to pinch me on the cheek, which used to annoy me when I was a kid but which I now thought was kind of cute.

"Have a good time at the party, baby," she said to Jennica.

Jennica nodded. "We will."

"Don't drink too much," her mother said, leaning in to kiss her on the cheek. "And call me if you can't drive."

I looked at Jennica in astonishment. But she merely nodded again, mumbled a goodbye, and grabbed my hand to drag me out the door.

"Bye!" Anne yelled behind us.

I waved, but I couldn't even muster the words to say goodbye. I was still in shock.

As soon as we got outside and the door was shut behind us, I exploded. "Your mom *knows* you drink?"

I knew Jennica sometimes drank beer when she was at parties or out with Brian, and I thought it was wrong. She could get in huge trouble! But she was always saying that everybody did it, so why shouldn't she?

"Yeah," Jennica muttered. She was looking at the ground. "So?"

"Soooo," I said, drawing the word out. "Don't you think that's weird?"

Jennica shrugged. "Whatever," she said. "She's cool, you know? She treats me like a grown-up now."

I just stared at her. I didn't even know what to say. What had happened to the old maternal, strict Mrs. Arroyo?

Jennica paused. "It's just been recently," she said. "Since my dad started dating the Spandex Leech. It's like my mom suddenly turned sixteen again. I found her in my closet one day, trying on my clothes, when I got home from school."

"That's so . . . weird," I said.

Jennica shrugged. "She seems happy. It's no big deal. It's cool." She paused awkwardly, cleared her throat, and added, "Anyways, let's go."

Without another word, she strode over to her mom's old Corolla, yanked open the door, and got inside. She slammed the door behind her and didn't look at me. It took me a second to snap myself out of it and join her. As soon as my door was shut, she started the car, threw it into reverse, and backed out of the driveway. She switched quickly to drive, cut the wheel sharply, and peeled out from the curb, like she couldn't get away from her house fast enough.

chapter 9

The party was in full swing by the time we got there. I followed Jennica and Brian toward the house, feeling more nervous than I usually did. Even though I'd been to parties before with Jennica, I knew I didn't belong. I didn't drink. I didn't have a boyfriend. I didn't make out with random guys. And I didn't really care whether people thought I was cool or not.

As we walked through the front door, we were blasted immediately by a wave of thumping bass turned up as loud as it could go. An old Kanye West song was throbbing from the speakers, and more people than should ever be crammed into any space were jostling and gyrating all over the Newells' perfect living room.

Most of the girls were dressed skimpily and were laughing too loudly and swaying a little bit on their stiletto heels. The boys were talking in unnaturally booming voices, slapping one another on the back and shamelessly ogling the girls. And everyone was carrying big red plastic cups filled with what I guessed was beer. In fact, I saw several people sloshing it onto the carpet as they talked.

Jennica turned to me with a big smile. "Isn't this *awesome*?" she asked, her eyes sparkling with enthusiasm.

"Um . . . ," I responded.

"Let's go get some beer!" she said loudly, close to my ear so that I could hear her over the music.

"I don't really want any!" I said back.

"What?" she shouted. I repeated myself, but she shook her head again. The music was too loud. I shrugged and followed her and Brian through the living room, out the French doors in the back. There was a line of about a dozen people waiting for beer while Scott Moore, who was in my English class, cheerfully pumped the keg handle. There was a couple kissing on the hanging swing near the house, and a stressed-out-looking senior girl, whose name I thought was Trish, was furiously texting on her phone while she chewed on her lower lip.

Jennica, Brian, and I got in line.

"Wassup?" Scott said as we got close to the keg. He grinned and handed us empty red cups. "Who's first?"

Jennica filled up her cup. "Your turn!" Scott told me as she stepped away from the keg and took a sip of her beer.

I hesitated. I'd always been so against drinking. But wouldn't it be nerdy to say no with a keg right in front of me?

Just then, I saw Sam come out of the house, scanning the yard. My jaw dropped. What was he doing here? At the same time, he caught sight of me, smiled, and waved. I ducked my head, immediately feeling guilty, like I'd been caught doing something wrong.

"Lacey?" Scott prompted, glancing at the growing line behind me. I snapped to attention and looked from him to the beer keg and back.

"Um, no thanks," I mumbled.

"You sure?" he asked.

"Yeah," I said. "I'm sure." Brian filled up and then slipped an arm around Jennica's waist.

"It's freezing out here," she said. I couldn't help noticing that she wrinkled her nose a little bit every time she sipped, like the beer tasted bad. Why would you drink something you didn't even like? "Can we go inside?" she asked.

I followed her and Brian back into the hot, loud, crowded living room. It felt like a sauna. A tall guy I didn't recognize splashed beer on me as he walked by.

"C'mon, Lacey!" Jennica shouted over the music. "Dance with us!" She took another big sip of her beer.

I shook my head and glanced around the room. I never should have come.

Just then, Logan and Sydney walked by, both of them clutching beer cups. From the looks of it, they'd been here for a while. One side of Logan's shirt was untucked, and his hair was a little messed up. I wondered how much he'd been drinking.

"Hey," he said when he saw me. "What's up?"

I could smell the beer on his breath. I shrugged. "Nothing." I glanced pointedly at the cup in his hand. Logan shifted it to his other hand.

"What are you doing here?" he asked.

"I'm with Jennica and Brian," I said.

Logan's eyes landed on my cup. "You're drinking?" he asked incredulously.

I realized it must look like I was holding a beer I'd finished, rather than one I'd never started. "So what if I am?" I asked.

"You don't drink," he said flatly.

I rolled my eyes. "I didn't think *you* drank either," I said.

"Yeah, well." He paused. "Maybe you don't know everything about me."

"Yeah, well," I said. "I guess I don't."

After I walked away from my brother and Sydney, I looked for Jennica and Brian, but I didn't see them anywhere. Amy Tan, from my trig class, told me she'd spotted them walking upstairs.

"To make out," she added unnecessarily. "Lots of people make out up there."

"Thanks," I said. "I've got it."

I felt more out of place than ever. I walked through the backyard, past the beer keg, past the handful of couples making out near the deck. The backyard was larger than I would have thought, and there was a small lake at the end of the lawn. I made my way down to the old wooden dock, pulling Jennica's cardigan more tightly around me as the wind whipped in stronger now that I wasn't shielded by the trees in the backyard anymore. I shivered, but I liked the feel of the breeze against my face.

I sat down on the edge of the dock, took off my strappy heels, and dangled my feet over.

The night was cold around me, and I was surprised at just how far away the sounds of the party seemed. It was quiet enough that I could hear crickets chirping and the occasional splash of a fish or a bird in the water. Across the lake, the darkness was punctuated by porch lights of houses, which looked much farther away than they did during the day

I was so tuned in to the sounds of the water that I didn't realize I wasn't alone until I heard a voice just behind me.

"I've been looking everywhere for you."

I jumped about a mile in the air and whipped my head around, my heart pounding double time.

It was Sam, standing there, looking down at me. He was backlit by the lights from the Newell house far behind us, and he seemed to almost glow in the shadows. I blinked a few times and tried to slow my racing heart. By the time my eyes adjusted, I noticed he had two cups, one of which he was holding out to me. "No thanks," I mumbled. "I don't drink."

Sam looked amused. "Me neither," he said. "All you need to do is take a walk through the party back there, and you realize how stupid it makes people act."

I looked at the cup again and raised an eyebrow.

He laughed. "It's not beer. It's Coke. I had a few cans in my Jeep."

I didn't know what to say. I took the plastic cup from his hand. "Oh. Thank you."

Sam sat down beside me, close enough that our thighs were almost touching. I could feel the heat from him. It made me shiver.

"So what are you doing down here?" he asked.

I shrugged and looked out at the water. "I don't know. I just wanted to be alone, I guess."

He seemed to consider this for a second. "Do you want me to leave?"

"No," I said, surprising myself with how quickly the word came out of my mouth. "I mean, that's okay. I don't care what you do."

"Why are you mad at me?" he asked.

"I'm not mad," I said.

"Was it something I said the other day?" he persisted. "When I drove you home?"

"Don't worry about it."

"Well, I *am* worried about it. You've been avoiding me since then. And I don't know what I did."

I squinted, wishing I didn't have to explain it to him. He'd never understand. "It's nothing personal. I just don't need another friend like you," I said.

He stared. "What do you mean?"

I gazed out at the lake without answering. After a moment, I felt his hand close over mine. It was big and warm and reminded me a little bit of the way my father's hand had fit around mine when I was little. I could feel my heart thudding in my chest.

"Please," he said. "Tell me what I did wrong."

I hesitated. His hand didn't move. And strangely, I realized I didn't want it to. "Look, I know I'm being dumb," I said. "But I didn't want to talk about my dad with you. I'm sick of having to explain it to people who have no idea what it feels like. Okay? Can you just drop it?"

He looked surprised and withdrew his hand. "I'm sorry."

"I'm just tired of people feeling sorry for me," I added.

"I don't feel sorry for you," Sam said.

"Whatever," I muttered. I paused. "And I hate it when people say they know how I feel. Okay? Because you don't know how I feel."

"Fair enough," he said. "I'm sorry. You're right. I don't know." He paused. "But I do understand, Lacey. Better than you think."

Our eyes met in the darkness, and he held my gaze. I blinked a few times. I didn't want to talk about this anymore. "So how come you don't drink?"

He gave me a half-smile. "First of all, I hate the taste of beer. Why would I drink something I don't like?"

"True," I said. I'd never had it, but it smelled terrible.

"It tastes like socks," Sam said, reading my mind. "Dirty socks."

I giggled.

"Plus, it makes people act like idiots."

I laughed. "True again."

"But the biggest reason, I guess, is that it's dangerous," he said. "Think about how many people in that house are going to drive home tonight. What if they get into an accident and get hurt or cause an accident that hurts someone else?"

I felt cold, the way I did whenever I thought of car accidents. Suddenly, I couldn't fathom ever wanting to drink anything in my entire life, if it could lead to something like that.

"I'd never drink and drive," Sam added.

"Me neither," I agreed. "No way."

I looked up at the sky. It was clear out tonight, with just a few wispy clouds drifting across the nearly full moon like pieces of gauzy silk suspended in space. I searched for the brightest star and recited the familiar words in my head: *Star light, star bright, first star I see tonight, I wish I may, I wish I might, have this wish, I wish tonight.* Then, without even thinking about it, I silently wished that Sam Stone would kiss me.

Immediately, I regretted it. I didn't necessarily believe in wishes coming true or anything like that, but what if they did? Shouldn't I have wished for my dad to be safe in heaven? Or for my mom to stop crying in her room at night? Or for Tanner to come out of his shell? Or for Jennica's mom to snap out of her weird teenager phase? What if I'd just wasted a wish? And why, of all the things I could wish for, would I wish for Sam to kiss me?

"So, I think I'm going to go," Sam said after a minute. "My mom worries when I'm out too late."

"My mom doesn't worry about anything anymore," I said before I could think about it.

Sam looked at me closely. "I bet she worries more than you realize."

I wanted to tell him that he had no idea what it was like in my family, and he had no idea what my mom was thinking. But there was something in his eyes that stopped me from speaking.

"Are you okay getting home?" he asked.

I hesitated. "I'm actually spending the night at Jennica's," I said.

"She's driving?"

I nodded.

"But she's drinking," Sam said. "I saw her."

I shrugged. "I'll figure it out," I said. "Don't worry." But I was worried. I didn't have my license, so I couldn't get us home, and there was no way I was climbing in a car with someone who'd had a few beers. I figured we'd have to call Jennica's mom, which I knew Jennica would argue with me about.

"How about I drive you home?" he asked. "You and Jennica and her boyfriend, I mean."

"You don't have to–" I started to say.

But he cut me off. "I'm not leaving you in a situation like that," Sam said firmly. He stood and pulled me up. "Let's go get her and tell her it's time to leave."

Sam didn't let go of my hand as he led me into the party and upstairs to find Jennica and Brian. Ten minutes later, his fingers were still intertwined with mine as the four of us walked out to the street to pile into Sam's Jeep. I realized I didn't want to let go.

chapter 10

The next morning, back to thinking about the conversation I'd had with Kelsi, I Googled "grief counseling for teens" and "starting a group for people whose parents have died." I read through all the entries, taking notes as I went, although there wasn't much I didn't know already. Most of the tips I found were pretty obvious, like letting everyone have a chance to talk and not pressuring anyone to open up.

Besides, I reminded myself, my goal wasn't to start some kind of grief group. I intended to make sure it was casual and not at all like the stupid counseling sessions Mom made us go to with Dr. Schiff. I was sure we'd all had enough of well-intentioned adults who didn't have a clue, who wanted to believe we were little kids they could fix with simple words from textbooks on grief.

I found a group in Atlanta called Kate's Club that sounded a lot like what I wanted to do. Kate was a woman in her thirties whose mom had died when she was twelve, and now she ran a group for more than a hundred kids. According to the group's Web site, they hung out together once a week, and once a month they did something fun, like go to a baseball game or to the aquarium. I imagined that one day I'd be like Kate. *Lacey's Club,* I thought.

But I was getting ahead of myself again.

I started an e-mail.

Hi, guys. Lacey Mann here. As you probably heard, Kelsi Hamilton's mom died last week, and Kelsi's back in school. I've been trying to figure out how to help her feel better, and then I realized that all of us could pitch in to make things easier on her. It might even help us, too. I was thinking that we could get together once in a while to hang out. We don't have to talk about anything if we don't want to. It's just a chance for us to feel like ourselves again and to hang out once in a while with people who get us. What do you think? Can you meet at the McDonald's on Samoset Street on Tuesday after school?

I thought about it for a moment. Then, I deleted *McDonald's* and typed in *Plymouth Diner*. It was only fitting that the place we'd meet for the first time would be the restaurant I thought of as belonging to me, my brothers, and Dad, the place we went for Saturday-morning pancakes. I hadn't been back there since the accident.

I sent the e-mail to Cody, Mindy, and Logan. Then I sent a different e-mail to Kelsi, telling her the plan.

After feeling so helpless at home, it felt good to finally be in control of something that had a real chance of helping people.

• • •

By Sunday night, there was still no word from any of the people I'd e-mailed. So I decided to call them.

"Hey," Cody said gruffly after his little sister handed the phone off to him.

"Hi, Cody. It's Lacey Mann. Did you get my e-mail?"

"Yeah."

"So? What do you think?" I asked. Cody and I didn't have classes together this year because I was in honors courses and he was in regular, but we'd gone to the same elementary school and junior high, and we knew each other well, even if we hadn't hung out in ages.

"I think it sounds kind of dumb," he said. "You want to get together just because we have dead parents? I mean, get over it, Lacey."

I took a deep breath. "I *am* over it, Cody. This is about Kelsi."

"So? What does that have to do with me?"

"Look," I said. "Let's just try this. Once. And if it feels stupid, you don't have to come again. But I just think it will be good for Kelsi to be around us now. Remember how weird it feels to have everyone treating you like you're some kind of alien?"

I could hear him breathing. "Yeah," he said in a low voice.

"I just think it would help if we could show her that there are people who know how she feels."

"So, what, are we supposed to talk about grief and stuff?" he asked. "I already had enough of that crap with the military psychologist my mom made us go to. It was stupid."

"No," I said. "No grief talk. Unless someone wants to."

There was another long silence. In the background, I could hear a television.

"Fine," Cody said finally. "But if it's stupid, I'm leaving."

"Okay," I agreed. We hung up, and as I placed the phone back in the receiver, I felt a little bubble of hope float up inside me.

I didn't know Mindy's number, so I called Kelsi next, and after a brief conversation about school stuff, I asked her if she was planning to come Tuesday.

"I guess so," she said. "Being in my house is depressing."

"I know the feeling," I said.

"My dad just cries all the time," she said. "Does your mom do that too?"

I hesitated. "No."

"I wish I could forget about it," Kelsi murmured.

"Yeah, me too," I said. Silence crackled over the line. "So how are you doing?" I asked. "I mean, really? Are you okay?"

"I guess," she said. "It's hard."

"Yeah," I said. "I know."

"So I'll see you at school?" she said.

I agreed, and we said our goodbyes. I mentally ticked Cody and Kelsi off my list. Two down. One to go.

A moment later, I was knocking on the door to Logan's bedroom.

"What?" His voice was muffled.

"I need to talk to you," I shouted.

"About what?"

"Can you just let me in?" I asked.

I heard a rustling, and then Logan pulled open the door, looking irritated. His room was dark, save for the light emanating from the monitor of his computer. An IM window was open. I figured he was probably talking to Sydney. Apparently, the world would end if they went more than a few hours without contact.

"What do you want?" Logan demanded, blocking the doorway.

"Can I come in?" I asked.

"Why? To snoop?" He didn't move.

"I just want to talk to you about Tuesday."

"Your stupid meeting thing?" Logan asked. I noticed that his eyes were bloodshot, which startled me. Had he been crying? The last time I'd seen his tears was Christmas morning, nearly ten months ago, when he'd come into the kitchen first thing in the morning and found me sitting alone there, staring at the wall, my hands wrapped around a mug of the Twinings Christmas tea that our dad used to drink all December. Logan had murmured, "He's really gone, isn't he?" before sinking into the chair across from me and starting to sob. He had cried, while I sat there, feeling uncomfortable, wondering why my own tears wouldn't come. From that day on, he had avoided looking me in the eye.

"It's not stupid," I said.

"Whatever," Logan muttered. "I don't see why we have to hang out with some girl I don't even know."

"Because it'll help her. So what's a couple of hours one afternoon if it makes her feel better?"

"Why do you have to save everyone, Lacey?" Logan asked. He raked his hand through his hair and shook his head. "I don't get you."

"I'm just trying to help."

"Yeah, well, you can do it without me," he said. "Some of us have better things to do." He slammed the door without another word.

chapter 11

Sam and I were different in class now. The time we'd spent together at the party had changed us. Or maybe it had just changed me by teaching me to relax a little and not judge him so harshly. In any case, we chatted easily before first period, and in sixth period, we worked together on an assignment, and he even showed me the picture he'd been doodling while Mr. Henchey droned on during the first ten minutes of class. In the time it had taken our teacher to explain our assignment, Sam had sketched him in pencil, only he had given him a Colonial soldier's uniform instead of normal clothes. I couldn't believe how good the drawing was.

"What, this?" Sam asked dismissively. He crumpled it up and looked embarrassed. "This is nothing. I draw a million of these a day."

By lunchtime on Tuesday, I was practically bubbling over with excited nerves about the meeting after school. Cody had nodded at me as we passed each other in the hall, and Kelsi had shot me a small smile.

"So can you help me with trig after school today?" Jennica asked as she and Brian plopped down across from me in the cafeteria.

"I can't," I said. "I've got that meeting after school today. Remember?" I'd told her about it on Saturday night when we went to the movies. I couldn't believe she'd forgotten.

Jennica looked at me blankly. "What?" she asked. "Oh, that death-group thing you're doing?"

"It's not a *death group,*" I said. "It's just some people getting together to support each other. And Kelsi."

Jennica nodded, and I could tell she was trying to look interested. "Yeah, sounds great," she said.

I tried not to let her forced enthusiasm bother me.

"It *is* going to be great," I said firmly.

"So who's going?"

I ticked off the short list.

"Pretty sad, huh?" she asked. "That there are that many kids whose parents have died?"

"Actually, in a school this size, I would have thought it would be more, you know?" I said.

Brian looped his arm around Jennica's shoulder and pulled her close. He whispered something in her ear and she giggled. It was like they'd both forgotten I was there.

As I dumped my tray and made my way alone toward the doors of the cafeteria, I looked up and saw Sam midway across the room, eating lunch with a small group of popular seniors. Summer was gazing at him from two seats away. But his attention wasn't on her. He was watching me.

Startled, I stopped for an instant longer than I should have. He raised his hand in a wave and smiled. Summer and a few of the others looked to see who he was waving at, then, apparently satisfied that it was no one important, they returned to their conversation.

• • •

As I walked down the street after school to the Plymouth Diner–about a half mile away–my heart was thudding so loudly that I was afraid everyone passing by would be able to hear it.

The restaurant was mostly empty, save for an elderly couple who were sitting on the same side of a booth, sharing an order of spaghetti and meatballs. I stood in the doorway for a moment, memories washing over me.

There was the booth in the back where we used to sit almost every Saturday; the waitresses knew to reserve it for us. I blinked a few times, images playing like a movie across the backs of my eyelids. Dad making airplane sounds and flying a spoon of oatmeal toward Tanner when he was little. Logan and Dad laughing and flinging whipped cream at each other from their strawberry pancakes, until a giant glob of white landed right on the tip of

Dad's nose. Dad cutting Tanner's fried eggs into bite-sized pieces. Dad putting his arm around me and giving me an affectionate noogie with his other hand while I complained, pretending to hate it, even though I couldn't hide my grin.

"Can I help you?" The hostess had appeared out of nowhere, someone I didn't recognize. But it had been almost a year since we'd last been here. I didn't know why I'd expected that the diner would be frozen in time, the way the memory of my dad was.

I asked for a table for five–just in case Logan and Mindy decided to show–and then waited nervously at the table.

The next seven minutes felt like an eternity. Finally a tiny girl with a mass of jet-black curls walked through the door and looked around, her eyes wide and unblinking. I recognized her immediately from her Facebook profile.

"Hi!" I exclaimed, hopping up. "Mindy?"

"Yeah," she said.

"Hey," I said. A tidal wave of relief washed over me as she stepped closer. "I'm Lacey Mann. I'm the one who organized this." I felt proud to say those words.

"Where is everyone?"

"You're the first one here."

"Oh." She hesitated.

"Here, sit down," I said before she could change her mind and bolt for the door. I couldn't think of anything to say. Not without everyone else here. I didn't want to get into anyone's stories without the whole group present.

"So you're a freshman, right?" I asked finally. The seconds ticked by.

"Yeah," Mindy said.

"You like Plymouth East so far?"

She shrugged. "I guess."

Just then, the door opened and Kelsi strode in. "Hey," she said, joining us. She sat down hard, throwing her book-laden backpack on the floor, where it landed with a loud thump.

Before I had the chance to say anything, the door opened again, and Cody came in, looking annoyed. "I'm here," he said. He was tall and a little stoop-shouldered with long, dark hair that flopped over his piercing dark eyes. He pushed a shaggy shock of hair behind his ears and ducked his head.

"Hi," I said. I felt immensely relieved; I realized I'd been expecting him not to show.

"This better not be dumb," he muttered. I felt a tight feeling in my chest. In my head, this had all gone so well; everyone would be glad to be here, we'd laugh together and cry together and feel better at the end. But now I was beginning to wonder just how dumb that was.

"So I guess we can get started," I said, suddenly unsure of how to begin.

"Whatever," Cody said. "Can't we order or something, though?"

We ordered Cokes and a few orders of fries to share. Just as we handed the waitress our menus, the door of the restaurant opened again, and Logan appeared in the slice of sunshine from outside, followed closely by Sydney. My jaw dropped.

"What's up, man?" he said to Cody as he strode over to our table. He nodded at Kelsi and Mindy, throwing a "What's up" their way, too. Since there was only one chair left, Logan grabbed one from another table and wedged it beside the empty one so that Sydney could sit next to him. She was eyeing me warily, a little smile on her face.

I could feel my blood boiling. "Logan, can I talk to you for a minute?" I asked, trying to keep my voice level.

He shrugged. "Whatever." But he allowed himself to be led away, back toward the entrance.

"I'm glad you came," I said evenly. "But what's Sydney doing here?"

"She's with me," he replied.

"I know *that,*" I said. "But this is a meeting for people whose parents have died. Sydney's mom and dad are fine!"

Logan shrugged. He knew he was bugging me. "Yeah, well," he said noncommittally.

"Can you maybe get rid of her for like an hour?" I asked. "And meet her after?"

Logan shook his head firmly, but I couldn't help thinking he looked a tiny bit guilty. He glanced toward the table, where Sydney was standing, hands on her hips, lips pursed, watching us with narrowed eyes.

"She wanted to come with me," he said. "And she's my *girlfriend.*"

"Yes, I'm aware of that."

Logan glanced at Sydney again and then back at me.

He lowered his voice. "Seriously, Lacey, can you loosen up a little?"

"Whatever," I muttered. I didn't have the energy to fight.

We made our way back to the table, and Logan whispered something in Sydney's ear. She giggled and the two of them sat down. Everyone looked at me expectantly. The waitress arrived with our Cokes, and Sydney and Logan ordered. I tried not to roll my eyes as Sydney asked for a sparkling water and a salad with low-cal dressing.

I took a long sip of my soda. "Hi," I said. "I know we all know each other, but I thought maybe we could start today by going around and introducing ourselves briefly and saying why we're here."

Cody snorted. "I thought you said this wasn't going to be like therapy."

"I already went to grief counseling," Mindy mumbled. "I hated it."

"Is that what this is?" Cody demanded. "Because if it is, I'm leaving."

"No," I said quickly. "It's not like I expect us to sit around and talk about death, you know?" I glanced at Kelsi, and she looked away. "But for today, I thought it would be a good idea if we at least all know each other's stories."

The smirk slipped from Cody's face. He looked down at his lap.

The rest of the group watched me in silence. I didn't think it was my imagination that Sydney looked uncomfortable.

"Fine, I'll go," I said finally. I took a deep breath. "I'm Lacey Mann. I have two brothers, Logan and Tanner. My dad died in a car accident last November. We were all with him in the car. All of us except for my mom, I mean."

I said the words matter-of-factly. I didn't expect them to make me feel weird, because it wasn't like they were anything new. These were all facts I had accepted. But there was a lump in my throat when I finished, and my eyes stung a little bit. "Logan?" I said. "Do you want to go next?"

"What do you want me to say?" he asked. "I have the same story as you."

"Duh," Sydney said under her breath.

"I just thought . . . ," I said. I stopped, because I wasn't sure *what* I'd thought.

"I'll go," Cody said. "I'm Cody. My dad died in Iraq when I was in eighth grade."

He paused, and I thought he was done. I was about to open my mouth to thank him when he spoke again.

"He was with his battalion," Cody continued. "It was just a normal day. They were driving along a road. And then all of a sudden, a bomb went off in the road in front of them. They had driven over some wire and tripped it. The bomb totally ripped apart the convoy. A few other soldiers were hurt. But my dad died. Right there."

He took a deep breath and then looked down at his lap.

It was Mindy who finally spoke. "That must have been really hard on you," she said. "To have him so far away. And not be able to say goodbye."

"Yeah, it sucked," Cody said. He paused. "What happened to your mom?"

Something inside me lurched. It was working. The people around the table were talking.

"She died," Mindy said simply. "Last year, when I was in eighth grade. She had been sick when I was younger. But the cancer went away, and we thought she was done with it. After a while, she stopped going to the doctor as often as she should have. And then, when they found it again, it was too late. It had already spread. She died really fast. I mean, in a couple of months. They tried chemo, but it didn't work. My little sister and I were with her. We had to move in with my dad after. He and my mom were divorced."

"Was he sad?" Kelsi asked in a soft voice.

"My dad?" Mindy asked, turning to her. Kelsi nodded. Mindy considered this for a minute. "I don't know. I never saw him cry or anything. He told me and my sister he was sad. But he's remarried. He has a new wife and a little baby now. I think it's weird for him that we live with him."

"Do you like your stepmom?" The question came from Logan. It surprised me that he was participating instead of mocking.

Mindy shook her head. "Not really. She's really young. She doesn't like us. Me and my sister, I mean."

"That must be hard," Cody said.

Mindy glanced at him. "Yeah," she said. "It is. We don't talk about my mom very often anymore. My dad gets uncomfortable when we bring her up."

I caught her eye. "You can talk about her here," I said. "With us."

Mindy smiled at me, a little sadly. "Yeah. I know."

"My mom died," Kelsi said in a tumble of words. "But you all know that. *Everyone* knows that. Don't they?"

There was a brief silence, then Cody laughed. It sounded out of place after her somber declaration. I looked at him, startled.

"Yeah, we're pretty much all famous," he said. To my surprise, Kelsi laughed too.

"Everyone knows you," Cody went on, "but no one knows what the heck to say to you."

"Sure they do," Kelsi said. She batted her eyelashes and adopted a high-pitched voice. "We're *so* sorry!"

We all laughed. I hadn't expected this. I was feeling better about this meeting idea every moment.

"Yeah," Mindy chimed in. "And then they just stare at you. And avoid you. Because they don't know what to say after that."

Everyone laughed except Logan and Sydney.

"That's not true," Sydney interjected. The laughter died down, and everyone looked at her. "People don't do that."

Cody narrowed his eyes. "Yeah they do."

"You're just being paranoid," Sydney retorted.

"Really?" Cody shot back. "And what makes *you* the expert?"

Sydney's face was turning red. "I'm just saying that I think you're all blowing things out of proportion," she said, her voice rising. She looked to Logan for support, but he was looking at his feet. "Besides, it's not like anyone means badly by it."

I hated to make things smoother for Sydney, especially

when she didn't belong here. But I also hated to have us fighting at the first meeting. So before Cody could reply, I cut in. "Sydney, I think Cody just means that people don't know how to act around us," I said. "Because they don't know what to say."

"Well, what are we supposed to do?" Sydney said. "Act like you're some kind of royalty or something? Just because you had one bad thing happen to you?"

I stared at her. "None of us expect to be treated like *royalty.* We just want to be treated normally. And it's not like having your parent die is just some random 'bad thing,' you know. It's a huge deal."

"Or maybe you're just *making* it a big deal," Sydney said. "Honestly, Lacey. I think this whole thing is a little silly. Don't you?"

She looked around the table, smirking, as if it were full of people who would agree with her. I was a bit heartened to see that Kelsi, Cody, and Mindy were staring stonily back at her. I opened my mouth to reply, but before I could, there was a deep voice from the direction of the doorway.

"I don't think it's silly at all."

We all turned to see who had come in unannounced. I practically fell out of my chair. Sam was standing by the hostess stand, his Red Sox cap pulled low over his forehead.

"Hey," he said, looking directly at me.

My heart was pounding, and my cheeks felt like they were on fire. "Um, thanks for saying that. But, um, what are you doing here? This is a group for people who have lost a parent."

Sam nodded slowly. "I know," he said. "That's why I'm here."

I was confused. I stared at him for a minute, uncomprehending.

"My dad," Sam said. He cleared his throat. "I lost my dad."

chapter 12

I couldn't believe it.

"Oh," I said. My cheeks grew even warmer. "I'm sorry. I didn't know." Suddenly, the conversation in the car came flooding back to me. Sam telling me he knew how I felt. Me getting defensive and mad. I felt a little sick.

Sam glanced at Sydney. "At my old school, everyone was weird to me. After they found out about my dad. I didn't want to have to deal with it with a whole new group of people when I moved here, you know?"

I knew exactly what he meant.

"I was trying to tell you," he said, looking straight at me. "That's what I was trying to say to you that day in the car."

"Oh." I swallowed hard.

"What happened, man?" Cody asked. "If it's cool for me to ask."

"A stroke," Sam said. "He had a stroke."

Sydney seemed to have been shamed into silence. The rest of us mumbled words of apology.

"Was it recent?" I asked. "With your dad?"

"Yeah," he said in a barely audible voice. "It was a few months ago. He just . . ." Sam paused, like he wasn't quite sure what to say next. He took a deep breath. "He was fine, you know? And then all of a sudden he wasn't. It was like something just went wrong in his face, like something short-circuited, you know, like a light that flickers all weird or something."

"You were with him?" Cody asked.

Sam nodded. "Yeah," he said. "I mean, I kept asking him what he was doing. I thought for a minute maybe he was joking, you know. But then I knew he wasn't. And I called nine-one-one."

Silence settled over us again.

"So, um, do you want to sit down?" I asked, clearing my throat.

"Yeah," Sam said. "I do."

• • •

Sydney left about five minutes after Sam joined the group. To my surprise, although he remained largely unresponsive, Logan stayed.

In the next hour, with me sort of leading the group, we talked a bit about our parents who had died, a little about what it was like with a whole new family dynamic, and what it was like when everyone at school treated you like a weirdo. But mostly, we just talked, awkwardly at first but then more like friends.

I learned all sorts of things I didn't know about people. Kelsi wanted to try out for softball this spring; Mindy had done gymnastics until her mom got sick and had even competed twice at the state level. Cody had just gotten a job at the local movie theater, tearing tickets, and he was thinking about signing up for the army next year, despite what had happened to his dad.

There were a million things I wanted to ask Sam, like when his dad had died and why his family had moved to Plymouth or how he seemed so much better adjusted. But unlike the rest of the group, he didn't seem to be volunteering any information. And I didn't want to make him uncomfortable. So I didn't say anything.

A few minutes later, after we had complained a little more about therapists and other adults who thought they knew exactly how we were supposed to feel, Cody looked at his watch and stood up. "I gotta go," he said. "My shift at the movie theater starts at four-thirty."

I checked my watch too. It was almost four. I couldn't believe we'd been talking for that long. It felt like just minutes ago that Sam had made his surprise appearance.

"Yeah, I guess we should get home," I said, glancing at Logan. I took a deep breath. "I am so glad all of you came today. I wasn't really sure how this would go. But I wanted, I don't know, a place for us to feel normal, you know?"

"A place for weirdos like us," Cody said. I thought for a split second that he was making fun of me until he winked and smiled.

"Yeah, weirdos like us," Mindy echoed. "I like that."

We all laughed.

"So, should we do this again?" I ventured after a moment. "Next week maybe?"

I held my breath.

Kelsi and Mindy exchanged glances. Cody shrugged. Logan didn't reply. But Sam was nodding enthusiastically.

"Yeah," he said. "I like that idea. Don't you?"

"Yeah," I said, glancing around.

"Yeah," Kelsi said. "That'd be cool, I guess."

"Okay," Mindy said.

"Whatever," Cody said. We all turned to Logan.

"I guess," he mumbled, looking down.

I couldn't stop the smile from spreading across my face. This was really going to work.

"Can I make a suggestion, though?" Sam asked. "What if we met somewhere else?"

"Like where?" Kelsi asked.

Sam smiled. "What if we went bowling?"

"Bowling?" Logan repeated.

"Yeah," Sam said. "Why not? My aunt Donna owns Lucky Strikes Lanes over off Main. I bet she'll give us a big discount. Or maybe she'll even let us bowl free."

"That sounds cool," Cody said.

I looked at the girls. I was worried that bowling would sound dorky and they wouldn't want to go. But they both nodded.

"Okay," Kelsi said.

I looked at Logan. He seemed annoyed, but he shrugged. "Yeah, whatever," he muttered.

I turned back to Sam and smiled. "That sounds like a good idea. So next Tuesday, then? A week from today?"

Everyone nodded.

"If anyone needs a ride, maybe we can just meet in the parking lot after school," Sam said. "I drive a Cherokee. I can fit a bunch of people."

"Okay, next Tuesday it is," I said. "And guys?"

Everyone looked at me, expectant. I paused.

"Thanks," I said finally. "Really. Thanks."

No one said anything for a minute. Then Mindy said softly, "Well, thanks for setting this up. It's nice to be someplace where you don't feel like a weirdo. Where you can feel like you did . . ."

Her voice trailed off. I knew exactly what she meant. But it was Kelsi who put it into words.

"Before," she filled in, her voice soft. "Where you can feel like you did before everything changed."

I beamed. This felt like the most important thing I had ever done. I was helping people.

"Thanks for coming," I said quietly.

And then, with a bunch of mumbled goodbyes, everyone went their separate ways. Sam glanced back and smiled at me as he walked out the door, but he didn't wait or ask if I needed a ride. A wall had gone up between us, and I'd been the one to put it there, all because I'd assumed that he was just like everyone else.

• • •

That night, Mom tried to get us to talk about the meeting, and I told her a little bit about it. Logan was strangely quiet, muttering only yes or no to Mom's questions. Tanner, as usual, pushed his food around on his plate and was silent. I felt a knot starting to form in my stomach as I looked around the table at my silent little brother, my sad-eyed mother, and grumpy Logan. For the millionth time, I missed Dad so much I could feel the pain in my chest.

After dinner, everyone shut themselves away in their rooms, even Mom. It made it feel like we were living in four separate little universes.

I did my trig homework at the dining room table, puzzling over one particularly complicated cosine problem. Then, closing my books, I walked upstairs and knocked on Logan's door.

"What?" he barked.

"It's me," I said. "Can I come in?"

There was a moment of silence. "Whatever."

I hadn't been in Logan's room in a while, and I was struck by how unfamiliar it felt. He had the same blue and green bedspread, of course, and the same white blinds that were a little bent on the lower right side. But he had taken down the surfing posters he used to have on his walls. In their place, he had a big collage made out of pictures of him and Sydney, with little hearts drawn all over it. Sydney had made it, of course, but I couldn't believe he had actually put it up.

He was sitting at his desk, shoulders slumped, staring at the bright screen of his computer. He had his history textbook spread in front of him and a few IM windows open.

"I, um, just wanted to say thanks for coming today," I said. I stood awkwardly in the doorway for a minute, then I crossed the room and sat on his bed. Logan sighed, typed a few things into the IM windows, and then turned around to look at me.

"Thanks," I continued after a pause. "For staying. After Sydney left, I mean."

"Yeah, well, now she's pissed at me," Logan said.

"Oh," I said. I didn't want to say that I was sorry, because I wasn't. "Well, maybe she shouldn't have been there in the first place."

Evidently, this was the wrong thing to say.

"Who are you to tell my girlfriend where she can and can't go?" Logan exploded.

"I'm not trying to do that," I said defensively.

"Whatever," Logan said bitterly. "You made her feel so uncomfortable. And now she's mad at *me*."

"Logan, I didn't do anything to make her feel uncomfortable," I said. "She got all defensive. Remember?"

"Yeah, well," Logan said. But he didn't continue.

We sat in silence. Then all of a sudden, Logan blurted out, "What's the point, anyways?"

I was startled. "The point of what?"

"Of your stupid club?" Logan asked. "What, like it's supposed to make us feel better?"

I shrugged. "I don't know. I just thought it might help. I thought today went well."

"Yeah, for you, maybe," he said.

I stared at him.

"You know, you say you hate that we feel different from everyone else," he said. "But then you start some group that makes us feel even *more* different."

"It's not supposed to make us feel like that," I protested. "It's supposed to give us a place to just feel normal."

"It's all about you, isn't it?" he said, an edge of bitterness creeping into his voice.

I couldn't understand why he'd say something like that. Everything I did these days was for other people. I worried about Mom. I tried to get Tanner to talk. I put up with Logan's stupid girlfriend just to keep the peace. "What are you talking about?" I asked.

Logan rolled his eyes. "I know, I know, you've been Saint Lacey since Dad died," he said. "But don't you ever get sick of being good? I mean, don't you just want to get pissed off at the world sometimes?"

"No," I said. How would that help?

Logan made a face. "Yeah, well, *I* don't always want to be perfect, you know? And Sydney doesn't want me to be."

He gazed at me triumphantly, like the fact that he had a "supportive" girlfriend was the answer to everything.

I stared at him for a minute. "How does Sydney even *know* what she wants, anyhow? She's so joined at the hip with you that I think you two are sharing a brain."

"Shut up, Lacey," he said. "You don't know everything."

I stood up. "Sometimes I don't think you know anything at all."

"You can't bring him back, you know," Logan said. "You can't bring anyone's parents back or make things like they were before. And it's stupid to try."

I stormed out of his room, slamming the door behind me. I went into my room, slamming that door too, and collapsed on my bed.

I waited for a minute, figuring that Mom would come to see what the problem was. After all, I was sure that the slamming doors could probably be heard down the block, especially since our house was so silent these days.

But she never came. And Logan didn't come to apologize. Instead, the loneliness settled down on me like a fog, and I lay slowly back on my bed, soaking in the silence.

chapter 13

After our Saturday-afternoon appointment with Dr. Schiff, Mom, Logan, and Tanner had once again shut themselves away in their rooms. Feeling lonely and bored, I called Jennica.

"Want to go to the mall or something?" I asked.

Silence. Then, "I'm busy, Lacey."

"With Brian?" I ventured.

"Not exactly," she replied. More awkward silence. Then she said, "Look. I found out on Thursday that my dad's getting remarried, okay? And things are just a little weird around here. I don't really feel like going to the mall."

I was stunned. "Your dad's getting remarried? To Leanne?"

"Yeah."

"I didn't know it was that serious," I said.

"Yeah, well," Jennica said. I could hear her sigh on the other end of the line. "There's a lot you don't know, Lacey."

I wondered what she meant. "But . . . why didn't you tell me?"

Jennica was silent for a minute. "I guess I didn't really expect you to understand."

"What?" Jennica and I talked about everything. Or at least we used to.

"Well, it's not like he's dead or anything," Jennica said. "I mean, you're always going on and on about how your life is so different because your dad died."

"I never talk about it," I interjected, surprised. I really didn't.

"Yeah, well," Jennica said. "I guess I just didn't expect you to take my problem that seriously."

"You're my best friend," I said. "Of course I'd take your problem seriously."

"Be honest," she said. "You think my thing is so much less important than yours, don't you?"

I hesitated. Part of me wanted to say yes, of course. No matter how sad she was, at least her dad was still alive. She still got to see him sometimes. Her whole world hadn't been shattered. Not the way mine had been. But I knew she didn't see it that way. And I knew that admitting that would be the wrong thing to say.

"Um," I said instead.

She made a muffled sound. "Like I said. Don't worry about it, Lacey."

And then, for the first time in our friendship, Jennica hung up without saying goodbye.

I sat down at the kitchen table and put my head in my hands. Jennica was mad at me. Logan barely talked to me. My mom was trying to put on a happy face, but she avoided the house and her kids as much as she could. And then there was Tanner.

I walked upstairs and knocked lightly on Tanner's door. He didn't reply, so I knocked again. "Tanner?" I called out. "Can I come in?"

I waited a minute, and hearing no reply, I pushed open the door.

The shades were drawn and the room was dark, even in the middle of the afternoon. The lamp beside Tanner's bed was on, but he was crouched in the shadows next to McGee's cage.

"Hey, buddy," I said. I crossed the room and knelt beside him. "How's it going?"

Tanner was staring into the cage like his life depended on it, his concentration entirely fixed. I glanced into the cage to see what McGee was doing.

Except McGee wasn't there. I bent my head to look inside his little plastic cave. No McGee. Nor was he on the hamster wheel. And the cage was small, only a few feet long and a few feet tall.

"Tanner?" I asked, starting to feel alarmed. "Where's McGee?"

Without looking at me, he raised his right arm and pointed toward the window.

"He's over by the window?" I asked.

Tanner shook his head.

I struggled to figure out what he meant. "He's outside?" That didn't make sense. "You let him outside?" But Tanner shook his head again. And then I noticed a tear roll down his right cheek. He blinked quickly and wiped it away as he went on staring at the empty cage.

Suddenly, I got it. "Tanner?" I asked. "Did McGee die?"

Tanner nodded once, still without looking at me.

"Oh, Tanner," I breathed, blinking back tears. "I'm so sorry. Why didn't you tell anyone?"

Tanner kept staring at the cage.

"Tanner, where is he?" I glanced toward the window. "Did you bury him out back?"

Tanner nodded again.

I swallowed hard. "Well, come on," I said resolutely. "McGee needs a proper funeral."

Tanner finally looked up at me, surprise playing across his face. "A funeral?"

An hour later, I had helped Tanner make a little cross-shaped headstone out of Popsicle sticks and glue. With a thin Sharpie he wrote "Good Bye McGee" on the horizontal sticks and drew a little picture of the hamster. While he drew, I downloaded "Amazing Grace"–the song that had played for much of our dad's funeral–on my iPod and grabbed my portable speakers from my room. Then, I got Mom and Logan and told them we needed to do something in the backyard.

Mom was mystified at first, but her face crumpled when I told her what had happened. She excused herself, and I could hear muffled sobs coming from her bathroom. Logan, on the other hand, just rolled his eyes.

"You're making me come outside for a *hamster's* funeral?" he demanded.

I glared at him. "No, I'm making you come outside to be supportive of our brother."

Looking annoyed, he got up and followed me downstairs, grumbling under his breath.

A few minutes later, we all stood under the old, arching oak tree in the left corner of the backyard, where Tanner had buried McGee. With a solemn look on his face, Tanner carefully stuck his Popsicle-stick cross in the ground and secured it with a pile of little pebbles. Then he stood up and pushed play on my iPod. The strains of "Amazing Grace" drifted through the yard, and as we all stood in silence, clustered around the tiny grave, the song and the solemnity of the moment reminded me uncomfortably of Dad's funeral. I gulped.

"Do you want to say a few words in McGee's honor?" I asked my little brother.

"Lacey," my mom said, "you know he doesn't like to talk. Don't push him."

But Tanner surprised us all by turning to face us and clearing his throat. "McGee was my friend," he began. I turned the iPod down a little. "He always understood me. He didn't try to make me talk. But he listened if I wanted to talk."

We stared at him. He hadn't spoken this much at a stretch since last November.

"He was just there for me," Tanner went on. He looked at the ground. "He was fun to play with. And I never had to talk about Dad or about being sad with him." He paused. "Thank you for coming to the funeral." Then before any of us could respond, he walked quickly away, toward the house. We stood and watched him in shocked silence until he disappeared into the house, pushing the door closed behind him.

• • •

After Tanner disappeared into the house, Mom went back to cleaning the kitchen, as if all her meticulous scrubbing and organizing could restore order to our lives, too. Sydney came and picked up Logan, who left without a word to any of us. And as our house fell silent again, I knew I had to get out.

I changed into running shorts, a sports bra, and a long-sleeved T-shirt and laced up the running shoes I hadn't put on in nearly a year. I used to love running, but I hadn't gone out once since the accident. At first, it was because my leg had been broken. But then, after it healed and after the doctors told me I should try to ease back into my normal routine, I couldn't bring myself to do it. Running made my leg ache, a dull, throbbing pain in the two places where the bone had been crushed. And the last thing I needed was a physical reminder of the accident.

But today, I wanted to feel it. I wanted to hurt. I wanted to feel *something*. And so I pulled my hair back in a ponytail, plugged earbuds into my iPod, and left the house without saying goodbye.

Evening was approaching, and with it, cooler temperatures. I shivered as I stretched in the driveway, but I knew that I'd warm up as I ran. I took off down the street, no particular route in mind. I pulled up Star Beck's latest album, the one she'd written herself, on my iPod, and let myself slip into the music as my feet pounded the pavement.

My leg ached, as I knew it would, every time my left foot hit the ground. I tried to imagine the exact places my femur had broken, tried to imagine the bone shattering as our car crumpled around us. It seemed unfair that my leg would be able to heal almost entirely, while my dad's injuries had stolen him in a matter of seconds. In a way, it was comforting that my leg still hurt, and I found myself wishing that it would ache more, as if hanging on to the pain of that day would give me a do-over.

I avoided, as I always did, the intersection where the accident had happened. It used to be part of my jogging route, but now I went the other way, winding deeper into our subdivision. I ran back toward the cranberry bogs, which were awash in red, ripe fruit. It was harvesting season, and even as the sunlight waned, I could see a few men in hip boots in what appeared to be a brick-colored sea, raking floating cranberries into containers. My dad had harvested cranberries as a side job when he was putting himself through college. I tried to imagine him out there with the other men, but I couldn't fix the image in my head. I used to be able to close my eyes and see the outline of his face so clearly, but now he had all but disappeared.

I turned away from the bogs. I ran along the main road for a little while, then dipped into the next neighborhood. Jennica lived here, and I ran by her house, not sure what I was intending to do or say. But the lights were all off, and her mom's car wasn't in the driveway. Perhaps she and her mother and sister had gone out to dinner, like a normal family.

I ran on. My leg still ached, but the pain felt like a companion now instead of a burden. I was running with it, not against it. I turned down a street I hadn't been on before and noticed, way off at the end, a guy in a long-sleeved gray tee, a baseball cap, and running shorts mowing the lawn of a big house that sat a little way up a hill. As I ran toward it, I thought about what an insurmountable task it seemed like with the push mower he was moving around the enormous yard. My feet took me closer, and just as I was about to pass by the house and loop down another street, the guy mowing the lawn turned, and I realized with a start that I knew him.

It was Sam.

I stopped in my tracks without meaning to, and our eyes met. He stared for a moment and then shut off the mower.

"Lacey?" he yelled down the lawn a little uncertainly.

"Um, hi," I said. I took my earbuds out and glanced around, unsure of what to do. I was suddenly conscious of how I must look. I was drenched in sweat, my hair was frizzing out of my ponytail, and I didn't have any makeup on, which meant that the two pimples on my chin were probably staring right at Sam, in all their angry red glory.

As Sam made his way down the lawn, I was surprised to see a tattoo on his left calf. I couldn't help staring. It was a Celtic claddagh, a pair of hands clasping a heart with a crown on top. My dad had the exact same one. I knew it meant love, friendship, and loyalty. My mother's wedding ring had the same design on it too, and my dad had once explained to me that it meant he had married his best friend, the woman he loved most in the world, and someone he'd be loyal to forever.

"You have a tattoo," I said.

"What?" He looked surprised and glanced down at his leg. "Oh. Yeah. I got it after my dad . . ." His voice trailed off. He looked down, then he smiled at me. "I thought my mom was going to kill me when I came home with it. The guy at the tattoo place thought I was eighteen."

I smiled. "My dad got a claddagh tattoo too. On his arm. He got it when he and my mom got married."

"Oh yeah?" Sam said. "That's cool."

We stood there awkwardly for a minute. "So," Sam finally said. "What are you doing here?"

I could feel the color rise to my cheeks. I probably looked like I was stalking him. "I was just going for a run," I said, and added hastily, "I had no idea you lived down here."

Sam glanced back at the house. "I'd invite you in, but my mom's sort of freaking out right now. My little brother just gave her his report card, and he failed English. They're screaming at each other. That's why I came out to mow the lawn."

"You have a brother?"

"Yeah," Sam said. "Joey. He's eight." He paused. "Is it just you and Logan?"

"I have another brother too," I said. "Tanner." I paused and added, "He's eleven. He doesn't talk very much anymore. Since the accident."

"It's crazy how much things change, isn't it?" Sam said. "You know, after."

"Yeah," I agreed. I suddenly wanted to change the subject. I glanced up at the lawn. "So you mow this whole thing by yourself?"

Sam laughed. "Yeah, it's crazy," he said. "Our old house had a much smaller yard, so it was a lot easier. But you know, I don't really mind. It's kind of nice to have a reason to be outside."

"I know," I said. Silence settled over us.

"So the other day was really cool," Sam said after a minute. "I mean, I think it was a really good idea."

I smiled. "Thanks."

Sam took off his cap raked a hand through his hair, getting a few tufts of grass stuck in his thick, dark strands. "Hey, could I run with you for a little while?"

"You want to run with me?"

He shrugged. "If that's cool," he said. "I used to run track at my old school. My dad was the coach, actually." A shadow flickered over his face.

"Sure," I said. "I haven't run in a while, though." I

paused. "Not since the accident, actually. So I'm not very fast."

"Good," Sam said. "Then you'll be easy to beat when I race you."

I laughed. He pushed the mower back up to the house and then jogged back down the driveway.

"You're not going to change clothes?" I asked.

He glanced down at his grass-stained sneakers, his faded running shorts, and his sweaty shirt. "Nah," he said.

We set off at a slow jog, and until we reached the end of the block, neither of us said a word. I was conscious of the silence between us and of my pounding heart, which was pumping blood so loudly that I feared Sam could hear it too. It wasn't until we were at the end of the street that Sam spoke.

"So do you have a boyfriend?" he asked.

Startled, I looked up at him. "Um, no," I said. I cleared my throat and focused on my pace. "Do you have a girlfriend?"

"Nah," he said. He paused and added, "I had one at my old school. But that was a while ago."

We jogged in silence again, and then Sam blurted out, "I think we should go out. You and me, I mean."

"What?" It sounded ruder than I'd meant it to.

"It's what I was trying to ask you that day in the car. Before you got mad. I think we should go out. Like, together."

I could feel myself blushing. "Really?" I asked. "Why?"

"You don't want to?" Sam asked. I noticed he wasn't looking at me, but his face seemed redder than it should have, considering that we weren't jogging that hard.

"No, no, I do," I said quickly. "I'm just not used to . . ." I didn't know what to say. What, that I wasn't used to guys liking me? That I wasn't used to being asked out? "You don't even know me," I finally concluded.

"What are you talking about?" he asked. "I sit next to you in two classes, and we've talked pretty much every day for the last month and a half."

"I guess," I said. I didn't know why I was being so reluctant. I was completely attracted to him; how could I not be? And I knew he wasn't asking me out just because he felt sorry for me or wanted to gossip about how great he was for taking out the poor little fatherless girl.

"Besides," Sam continued, "how are you going to get to know me if you don't let me take you out to dinner?"

"When?" I asked.

"Tomorrow night?" he said.

I thought for a minute. "Yeah," I said. "I could do that."

We both fell into silence again, and as I ran, my mind swirled, thinking about the fact that at this time tomorrow, I'd actually be out with Sam Stone. Who was hot and sweaty–and really, really gorgeous–as he jogged next to me right now.

"So tell me about your little brother," Sam said as we turned out of his neighborhood onto Long Pond Road.

I hesitated, then began to tell him about how much Tanner liked animals and video games and how he used to love searching for the prize in the bottom of the Cracker Jack boxes at ball games. And before I knew it, I found myself telling Sam about Tanner's almost constant silence and how much it worried me. He told me that he was really scared to see his brother withdraw from everything he used to love. And I was surprised to realize that our mothers seemed to have reacted to losing our fathers the same way: by throwing themselves into their work and social lives instead of spending time with us.

"It's like she thinks that if she just works hard enough, she can forget," Sam said, glancing down at me.

"That's exactly how my mom is too," I said. Somehow, it helped to know that my family wasn't the only one crumbling, the only one where the remaining adult had retreated rather than dealing.

It was the best conversation I'd had since the accident.

As we jogged and talked, our feet eventually carried us to my house, like that's where we'd been going all along. By the time we got there, we'd covered everything from Jennica to Sam's best friend Chris at his old school who didn't call anymore to how hard it was to come into a close-knit community like this one and make friends, when everyone had known one another since preschool.

We stopped in my driveway, and as we stood catching our breath, I asked, "Do you want to come in and get some water or something?"

Sam looked at his watch. "Nah," he said. "My mom's probably wondering where I am. I'd better get home."

"Want me to get my mom to drive you?" I asked. Then I added apologetically, "She won't let me drive, even though I'm sixteen. It has to do with the accident."

Sam nodded, like he understood and wasn't going to judge me. "Nah, I'm good," he said. "I should be able to make it home in twenty minutes if I pick up the pace a little."

"You saying I'm slow?" I teased.

He laughed. "No. I'm saying I enjoyed our conversation too much to put any thought into actually running."

Then, before I realized what was happening, he leaned down and gave me a quick peck on the lips. He pulled back, looking embarrassed, before I could get my mouth to unfreeze long enough to reply.

"Pick you up at six," he said.

He was already disappearing down the street before I raised my hand in a silent goodbye. My lips were still tingling as he vanished around the corner.

chapter 14

I practically floated up to my bedroom and booted up my computer. After a quick shower to rinse my hair and wash the run away, I went online. Jennica's screen name popped up in a little IM window, accompanied by her AIM tone, which was the sound of a kiss.

JENNICAJENNICA: Hey Lacey.
JENNICAJENNICA: I'm sorry.

I gulped. I paused and typed back.

LACEYLOO321: it's ok
JENNICAJENNICA: i was a jerk.
LACEYLOO321: u weren't a jerk.
JENNICAJENNICA: i was.
LACEYLOO321: weren't
JENNICAJENNICA: was
LACEYLOO321: agree to disagree?
JENNICAJENNICA: only if u accept my apology.
LACEYLOO321: deal.
LACEYLOO321: :-)
LACEYLOO321: hey, i'm sorry u r upset about ur dad.
JENNICAJENNICA: :-(
JENNICAJENNICA: it's no big deal.
LACEYLOO321: yeah it is. i shouldn't act like it's not. i'm sorry if i do that.
JENNICAJENNICA: it's ok.
JENNICAJENNICA: besides. it's not a big deal. not like ur dad. i know that, ok?
LACEYLOO321: i don't want to talk about that.
JENNICAJENNICA: u never do.
JENNICAJENNICA: is that what you talked about at ur group? that group for kelsi?
LACEYLOO321: not really. we just kinda hung out.
JENNICAJENNICA: why? they're not even ur friends.
LACEYLOO321: i dunno. it's just nice. to have people who understand you.
JENNICAJENNICA: i understand u.
LACEYLOO321: i know.

JENNICAJENNICA: but u don't talk to me.
LACEYLOO321: it's different w/ people who have lost a parent 2.
JENNICAJENNICA: but i try to understand.
LACEYLOO321: i know.
LACEYLOO321: . . .
LACEYLOO321: maybe i don't give you enough credit for that.
JENNICAJENNICA: so anyway.
JENNICAJENNICA: my dad's stupid wedding is in 2 months.
LACEYLOO321: what????!!!! 2 MONTHS???? but he just got engaged!!!!!!!!!!!
JENNICAJENNICA: ya
LACEYLOO321: that's CRAZY.
JENNICAJENNICA: ya
JENNICAJENNICA: i hate his stupid girlfriend.
LACEYLOO321: she's like our age.
JENNICAJENNICA: almost. she's like 23 or something.
LACEYLOO321: what does brian think?

There was a long pause. I thought maybe Jennica had signed off without seeing my last question. I was just about to close the IM window when she wrote back.

JENNICAJENNICA: he thinks i'm being dumb
LACEYLOO321: what????
JENNICAJENNICA: i dunno
LACEYLOO321: are u 2 fighting?

JENNICAJENNICA: not exactly. kinda.
LACEYLOO321: about what???
JENNICAJENNICA: he doesn't get it
JENNICAJENNICA: his dad is on wife #3. and his mom just got married last year
LACEYLOO321: so?
JENNICAJENNICA: he just doesn't think it's a big deal. doesn't get why i'm upset.
LACEYLOO321: that's crazy
JENNICAJENNICA: yeah. well.
LACEYLOO321: i'm sorry.
JENNICAJENNICA: ya. thanx.
JENNICAJENNICA: gotta go. my mom's yelling at me.
LACEYLOO321: hey, i've got something to tell you.
JENNICAJENNICA: can we talk tmrow? seriously, mom's pissed.
LACEYLOO321: yeah. u ok?
JENNICAJENNICA: ya. see ya. can u come over tmrw? like lunchtime? we can go to the mall.
LACEYLOO321: yeah. c u at noon?
JENNICAJENNICA: c u. bye!

• • •

"We're not invited to the wedding," Jennica told me as she opened her door the next day.

"What?" I asked, my heart aching for her. "You're not?"

Jennica nodded. "My dad's *fiancée*"—she spat the word

out like it tasted terrible—"is apparently afraid Anne and I will make a *scene.*"

As much as Jennica disliked her dad's bride-to-be, a spandex-wearing, yoga-practicing blond waif who was the polar opposite of Jennica's dark-haired, pleasantly plump Cuban American mom, she and Anne had been raised to be polite in every situation. I knew as well as her father did that Jennica would never, in a million years, make a scene at someone's wedding—even if she hated the person.

"But what about your dad?" I asked. "Isn't he insisting you come? I mean, he's your *dad*!"

Jennica's eyes filled with tears, which she wiped away angrily, as if furious that they were even there in the first place. "No." The word sliced out of her mouth.

"No?"

"No," she repeated. "He says it's Leanne's day. And he wants it to be perfect for her."

"But it's his day too," I protested. "And you're his kids."

"Yeah, well." Jennica shrugged. "I guess that doesn't matter."

"He still loves you, Jennica," I said. I knew the words were weak. I didn't know what else to say.

"Well, it doesn't feel like it."

I thought about my family and about how far apart we'd all drifted. I thought about my dad, and how he wasn't here for us when we needed him most. And weird as it was, I thought about Sam and the fact that in just a few minutes of talking to him, he'd made me feel more understood than I'd felt in the last ten months.

"My mom's out and Anne's at her friend's house," Jennica said, changing the subject. "Is it cool with you if we just go to the mall now and eat there? I promised I'd have the car back by three."

"Sure," I said.

It wasn't until we were walking into Macy's that I blurted out, "So I'm going out with someone tonight."

Jennica stopped. "Who?" she practically shrieked.

"Sam Stone."

"What? Since when? Why didn't you tell me?"

"I'm telling you now." I quickly recounted the story of my jog yesterday and of running into him as he mowed his lawn.

"He's, like, completely gorgeous," Jennica said. "I can't believe you're going out with him."

"I know," I said.

"Omigod," Jennica said.

"I know," I repeated with a smile.

"Well, we totally have to get you a new outfit, shoes, a top, earrings–"

"It's not really that big of a deal," I protested. I felt silly. "I mean, it's a Sunday night. We're just going to dinner."

"And you need to look hot."

For the next hour, Jennica seemed to forget entirely about her dad's upcoming remarriage as we raced around the mall. She was on a mission as she rifled through sale racks, throwing dresses, skirts, and cute tops at me. And she was chattering a mile a minute.

"So you have to ask a lot of questions, but not too many, because you want to seem interested, but not annoying," she rambled. "And you want to make eye contact, but you can't, like, stare, because that comes off as creepy, you know? And you should order a real meal, not just a salad, because guys don't like girls who don't eat, but you shouldn't finish it all, because you don't want to look like a pig. And you should remember to cross your legs, bat your eyes, and sometimes lick your lips, because it's been proven that guys find that attractive."

"Jennica," I said after we got our lunch and found seats in the crowded food court, "I appreciate all the advice. But I think I'm just going to be myself."

"Be yourself?" Jennica repeated. She looked horrified.

"I'm not a total loser or anything," I said, taking a bite of my hot dog.

"No . . . but you aren't exactly used to going out with cute guys."

I gave her a look. "I think I can manage."

Jennica took a sip of her soda. "You are going to have so much fun. I'm actually kind of jealous."

"What, of me going out with Sam?" I asked, surprised.

"No," she said. "Of how excited you are."

"Don't you feel like this with Brian?" I asked.

Jennica paused. "No," she said. "Not anymore."

chapter 15

When the doorbell rang, I took one last look in the mirror, then raced downstairs. I'd bought a new black top with a deep pink rose stitched up the side, and I'd paired it with my favorite jeans, black boots, and gold hoop earrings. I looked good.

"Hey," Logan said, beating me to the door. He stared at Sam, who looked ridiculously hot in dark jeans, a white button-down shirt, and his leather jacket.

Sam looked past Logan and saw me coming down the stairs. "Hey." His smiled widened.

"Tell Mom I'll be home by ten," I told my wide-eyed brother.

• • •

We ate at a place called Saltwinds, which looked out over Plymouth Bay. And luckily I didn't need Jennica's rules–I didn't even feel nervous. It was like talking to a friend who happened to be super cute.

"I want to show you something," Sam told me after dinner. "Do you have another couple of hours?"

I doubted Mom would even notice if I was late. "Yeah," I said.

Sam turned east on Route 44, but I didn't figure out where we were going until we were well outside the city limits.

"Are we going to where you used to live?" I asked.

"Near there," Sam said mysteriously.

Just after we passed a WELCOME TO TAUNTON sign, Sam took a left and then another left onto a dirt road. We drove until I could see a collapsed bridge across a river ahead of us.

"You're not going to try to cross that or something, are you?" I asked, realizing as I said it that I was being silly.

"No," Sam laughed. "Just trust me, okay?" He pulled off the dirt road and parked several yards from the water. He shut off the ignition and crossed around to the passenger side to help me out. "Come on," he said. "It's not muddy."

I hopped out of the Jeep. He took my hand, lacing his fingers through mine the way he had at the party. We walked in silence under the bridge. I looked at the water, half expecting to see a boat or something down there. But when we reached the bank, Sam gently put his hands on my shoulders and turned me around so that I was facing the underside of the bridge.

I stared without speaking. I didn't know what to say; it was like nothing I'd ever seen.

The entire underside of the bridge abutment was painted with a mural in all the colors of the rainbow. Every available inch of space was filled with individual scenes. Kids played together; families sat around the dinner table; stars sparkled in the sky.

"Wow," I said. "This is amazing."

"It's where I used to come before we moved to Plymouth. You know, when I needed to get away," Sam said.

"How did you find this mural?" I asked.

Sam laughed. "Find it? I painted it."

I looked at him in disbelief. "What?"

He looked a little embarrassed. "I mean, it's not that big of a deal. It's just how I get stuff out, you know? Like this." He walked over and pointed to a scene of three people standing together, their backs to us. The man in the middle was pointing upward. The boys to either side of him, one younger than the other, were looking in the direction of his finger. "This is the first thing I painted. It's my dad and my brother and me when we were little. He used to take us to the air show in Chicopee. For some reason, after his stroke, this was the image I couldn't get out of my head."

"It's beautiful," I said. I reached out and touched the paint, feeling its texture beneath my fingers.

"And this"–he walked me a few feet to the right, where a man and a woman knelt laughing under a Christmas tree–"was the Christmas that my dad gave my mom a pair of socks and then surprised her by pulling a necklace out of his bathrobe pocket while she was trying to pretend she liked the socks."

He took me down the mural, pointing out scenes here and there. I couldn't get over the level of skill; some of the figures looked real enough to reach out and touch. As Sam talked me through some of the pictures, I couldn't help feeling like I was reading the CliffsNotes to his life. I liked it.

After a while, he led me over to a cement block near the river, and we sat down.

"So, you never told me what happened to your dad," he said after a minute. He reached for my hand and squeezed. "You don't have to talk about it. But if you want to, I'd like to hear."

I looked down at the water. "I'm sure you've heard the story," I said. "Everyone at school talks about it."

"I don't listen to rumors," Sam said.

I took a deep breath. "Okay." I looked up and cleared my throat.

"It happened last November," I began. Slowly, I told him about that crisp, bright autumn morning eleven months ago, when everything in the world had seemed so perfect. The words poured out, as they'd never done before. No one had ever asked for my story; everyone assumed they already knew.

"The worst part about it is . . ." I couldn't finish the sentence. Sam put his hand on my shoulder, and I knew he was trying to comfort me. I couldn't meet his eyes. "I think it was my fault," I said, so softly that I wasn't sure Sam could even hear me.

"It *wasn't* your fault," he said right away.

"Yeah, it was." I still couldn't look at him. "Sam, if I hadn't spent that extra time in the bathroom, if I hadn't been so stupid and shallow"–I took a deep breath–"my dad would still be here."

"Lacey," Sam said firmly.

I continued to look down. I swallowed the lump in my throat.

"Lacey," Sam repeated. "Look at me."

His face was inches from mine. I could feel his warm breath. He was looking at me intensely.

"What?" I whispered

"It wasn't your fault," he said.

"But it was," I said. "If I had just taken less time–"

"No."

"But if I had screamed or something when I saw the other car–"

"No, Lacey."

"If I hadn't been dragging my feet to annoy Logan–"

"No," Sam cut me off, his voice leaving no room for argument. "It was *not* your fault. Just like it wasn't my fault with my dad. I beat myself up about it for a while, Lacey.

Even after the doctors said there wasn't anything I could have done. But it wasn't me. And it wasn't you. And as unfair as this is, and as hard as it is to understand, it was just their time for something to happen."

I swallowed hard. I didn't believe that. How could it have been my dad's time? He was thirty-eight. Just the other day, we'd read in history class about a man in Puerto Rico who had lived to be 115. How was that possible? He had lived three of my father's lifetimes.

I stared out into the blackness for a while and tried to process what Sam had said. He had felt like it was his fault too when his dad died. But what could he have done to stop a stroke?

It was different for me. There were a thousand things I could have done to change the outcome that day. I could have gotten up earlier that morning. I could have taken less time in the bathroom. I could have chosen not to deliberately annoy Logan. I could have looked up a second sooner in the car and seen the SUV barreling toward us. I could have warned my dad before it was too late.

If I'd done any of those things, my dad would still be alive.

But I knew Sam wouldn't understand that or would try to talk me out of it, the way Dr. Schiff did whenever we touched on the topic. So instead, as I did with her, I changed the subject. "The anniversary is in three weeks," I said. I looked out in the blackness of the night and tried to focus on one of the porch lights across the river. Sometimes, if I stared into the darkness long enough, I could see the shape of my dad's face in the shadows, his familiar form coming out of the blackness. But not tonight.

"The anniversary of the accident?" Sam asked.

I nodded. "November fifteenth," I said. "It's weird thinking it's been a whole year."

Sam slipped his arm around my shoulder and scooted a little closer so that the sides of our bodies were pressed together. I should have felt nervous, or at least that tingly, anticipatory feeling of being with someone I really liked. But instead, all I could think about was my dad.

"You must miss him," Sam said, his breath tickling my ear.

I nodded and he gave my shoulder a long squeeze, pulling me closer. "So much has changed," I said. "I miss him more than I could even say. But I miss *us,* too. I miss my family. I miss being normal. I miss the sound of my little brother's voice. I miss seeing my mom smile. I miss being able to feel happy, even for an instant, without feeling guilty."

I paused, embarrassed, and looked at Sam. "I'm glad you're here," I said. "I've never been able to talk to someone who understands before. I mean, I know other people whose parents have been sick or have had cancer or who have gotten divorced. And that's really sad. But it's not the same thing. Talking to you just makes me feel safe."

Sam shifted, and I thought he was going to say something, but he didn't. I settled back against his shoulder and gazed out at the river.

"Sometimes, I miss my dad so much it literally hurts,"

I whispered. I wasn't even sure I'd said the words aloud until I felt Sam's arm tighten around me.

"I know," he said. "Can I show you something?"

He led me back to the mural, to the far right side, and pointed up, above the heads of the paintings of himself and his mom and brother watching a baseball game. "See that rainbow?"

Sam had painted a sunny sky with only a few wisps of clouds. But in the middle of it, so faint that you had to strain to see it, there was the lightest wash of red, orange, yellow, green, blue, and purple, all in an arching ribbon of translucent color.

"My uncle Joe died when I was ten. Cancer," Sam continued. "We were all really close, so it was really tough on me."

"I'm sorry," I said.

Sam shook his head. "No, it's okay. But my point in telling you is that my dad used to say that anytime we could see a rainbow in the sky, that was Uncle Joe telling us he was all right."

"A rainbow?" I asked.

Sam shrugged, embarrassed. "I know it sounds dumb."

"No, it doesn't," I said gently. "But do you believe that? I mean, really believe it?"

"I didn't at first. But you know, I started noticing that there were rainbows in the sky at the weirdest times. Like the afternoon my dad had his stroke. It wasn't even rainy that day. But I swear, when we got to the hospital with the paramedics, I looked up, and there was this really faint rainbow in the sky."

"Really?"

"Maybe it's not as crazy as it sounds. I mean, if you believe in heaven and all."

"I do," I said simply. You had to believe in heaven when your dad died. The alternative, that your father's soul simply vanished, was too awful to even consider.

"So what I meant was, I think maybe your dad's been here all this time," Sam said. "Maybe he does see you. You just haven't known where to look for him."

I nodded quickly. I was trying to fight a strange feeling welling up inside me. It almost felt like I was going to cry, but I hadn't done that in almost a year. Not since that day in the cafeteria with Tali and Tatiana. It wasn't that I didn't want to. But every time I felt like the tears should come, they didn't. This was the closest I'd felt. My insides swam uncomfortably. I fought the feeling. I didn't want to cry; I couldn't afford to crack now, for so many reasons.

"Thanks," I said finally.

I looked back at the mural and realized that the figures of Sam, his mother, and his brother weren't watching the baseball game after all. They were looking up at the rainbow, which seemed to rise out of the horizon, behind Fenway Park's Green Monster. I smiled at Sam. He was already staring at me, and for a moment, we just held each other's gaze.

I knew it was going to happen a second before it did. Our breath grew short. The space between us grew smaller. And then, Sam's hand was on my cheek, brushing it gently. When he finally leaned in and touched his lips to mine, my eyes were already closed, and I was already leaning toward him.

Sam tasted a little like Coke, but sweeter. As our lips touched, it was like someone had cranked up all my senses. I could smell something burning in the distance and the leaves turning to fall and the almost imperceptibly salty smell wafting in from the river. I could hear the chirping of the crickets and the splashes of the water and a train whistle in the distance. And Sam's hand touching my cheek ignited every cell in my skin.

We kissed for a long time without saying anything.

Finally, Sam pulled back a little.

"Wow," he said, his nose still just a couple of inches from mine.

I smiled. "Yeah," I agreed.

Sam kissed my forehead. "Mind if we just sit here for a while?"

"Nope," I said.

Together, we turned and looked out into the darkness.

chapter 16

Forty minutes later, we were pulling into my driveway. I didn't want the evening to end.

"I had a great time with you," I said.

"Me too," Sam said. He paused. "Listen, Lacey, I need to tell you something."

I turned to him. He looked worried. And all of a sudden, I realized that whatever it was, I didn't want to hear it tonight. I didn't want anything to ruin our perfect night.

"Tell me tomorrow," I said.

"But–"

"Is it that you have some girlfriend back in Taunton or

something?" I asked, trying to sound like I was making a joke. But I meant it, actually. It would be just my luck to have truly connected with the perfect guy and to find out he was keeping something huge hidden from me.

Sam laughed. "No."

"Then can you tell me tomorrow?"

He nodded. I looked out the window at my front lawn, which was covered in a blanket of autumn leaves in varying shades of orange, red, and yellow, illuminated under the shallow glow cast by the streetlights. They reminded me of the first three colors of Sam's rainbow.

"My dad used to rake the leaves and make a big pile for all of us to jump in every fall," I said. "Even when we were too old for it. Even Logan and I would jump in."

"That sounds really nice," Sam said.

"Is it weird that I miss things like the leaf pile, instead of just missing my dad?" I asked.

"It's not weird at all," Sam said. He leaned across the center console and touched his lips lightly to mine. We lingered there for a minute, our lips just barely touching. Finally, he pulled back and looked me right in the eye again.

"Lacey Mann," he said, "you're pretty amazing."

I smiled. "You're not so bad yourself, Sam Stone."

He grinned. "See you tomorrow, then?"

"See you tomorrow."

Sam walked me to my front door and after one last, quick kiss, I said goodbye and turned the key quietly in the lock. I smiled once more at Sam before shutting the door behind me. As I tiptoed up the stairs, avoiding the steps that creaked, I thought about how one day could make such a difference in your life. A year ago, it had been losing Dad—and my family—in a morning, in the blink of an eye. But today, it had been finding something new with Sam that I had the feeling would last for a long time.

• • •

At school now, everything was different. Even though we'd never said the words, never officially made some sort of declaration of togetherness, Sam and I were a couple.

It was strange. I'd never had a boyfriend before. And I certainly wasn't used to people staring at me in the halls with jealousy in their eyes instead of pity. It was kind of nice to be the center of a different kind of attention.

I figured at first that Logan and Sydney must have gossiped about me and Sam, but as the day went on I realized that we were creating our own waves. And although we had agreed on the disgustingness of Jennica-style PDA, Sam didn't seem embarrassed in the slightest to greet me in trig class with a peck on the cheek, like we'd been dating forever, or to walk me to my locker after class with my bookbag slung over his shoulder. He ate lunch with me, Jennica, and Brian and seemed completely oblivious to the stares from other tables.

"So is Sam, like, your boyfriend now?" Jennica whispered as we went to throw out our trash. Brian and Sam were several paces behind us, talking about the Patriots game this weekend.

"I don't know," I said. "I guess so. It's weird."

"That happened fast."

The words unsettled me, because I wasn't exactly sure what she meant. "What do you mean?"

She shrugged. "Sometimes relationships that develop so quickly aren't really based on anything real."

I wondered whether she was talking about me or about her dad and Leanne.

"But he seems to really like you," she added hastily, as if she'd just realized what she'd said and how it had sounded. "I'm sure things are fine."

• • •

The next afternoon was supposed to be our second group meeting. I'd been so caught up with thinking about Sam over the weekend that I hadn't even sent out a reminder e-mail. I spent the whole day feeling guilty that I had dropped the ball. It was so unlike me.

I waited in the parking lot after school, near the fence around the football stadium, wondering who would show up for a ride. Sam had offered to drive everyone last week, and he had reminded me in sixth period today. Logan hadn't said one way or the other whether he was coming, but I figured that if he did show up, he'd get a ride from Sydney. That left Mindy, Kelsi, and Cody.

Five minutes after the final bell, I saw Sam striding out, his Red Sox cap and leather jacket on, as usual. His bag was slung over his shoulder, and he was grinning as he approached.

"Hey you," he said as he reached me. "You ready to go?"

I fell into step beside him. "We should probably wait and see if anyone else needs a ride."

"Sure thing," he said cheerfully as we reached his Jeep.

Sam started the engine, fiddled with the heat for a minute, and then pushed Play on his CD player. A song I recognized from my dad's CD collection started playing.

"You like Jimmy Buffett?" I asked, surprised. I didn't know anyone else our age who did. I'd always liked "Cheeseburger in Paradise" and some of his other songs. My dad used to make goofy faces when he sang along.

Sam seemed equally surprised. "Yeah," he said. "You know Buffett?"

I nodded. "My dad really liked him."

"Yeah?" he said. "My dad too." He smiled a little. "He was actually a Parrothead. Official member of the Jimmy Buffett fan club."

I laughed. "Same with my dad!"

"Did he go last time Jimmy played at Gillette Stadium?"

"Yep."

"So did my dad," Sam said. "Isn't it weird to think that they sat in the same stadium at the same show? And we hadn't even moved here yet?"

"Yeah," I said. Actually, I thought, it seemed stranger to me that there existed a time, in the not-so-distant past, that my dad and Sam's dad had been out enjoying a rock concert, maybe just rows away from each other, with no idea that their days were numbered. It made me feel so suddenly sad that my throat closed up. I glanced at Sam, and the smile had fallen from his face too. I wondered if he was thinking the same thing.

After a few minutes of waiting, the crowd of students flowing out from the school had slowed to a trickle, and the parking lot was nearly empty. Sam checked his watch. "Think everyone found a ride?"

I nodded and took a deep breath, which I exhaled in a nervous laugh. "Actually, I'm really worried that no one will show up at all."

"Why?" Sam asked.

I shrugged. "I don't know. Maybe everyone thought last week was really stupid. I mean, maybe they thought about it later and realized they didn't want to hang out again with a bunch of sad people."

Sam seemed to think about this for a minute. "No," he said firmly. "I know it helped. And I know people felt good about it."

"Are you sure?" I asked in a small voice.

"Yes," Sam said. We waited another few minutes, the silence hanging over us, then Sam shifted into drive. "I guess we should go."

I nodded, feeling discouraged. What if it *was* just me and Sam? I'd feel like such a failure. And I'd look like an idiot.

As we drove, I glanced at him a few times out of the corner of my eye when I knew he was paying attention to the road. I liked how angular his face was from the side. Sharp nose, sharp chin. But he didn't seem sharp-featured when you looked straight at him. It was funny how different people could appear when you simply looked at them from different angles.

When Sam and I pulled into the Lucky Strikes parking

lot it was almost totally empty. There was a beat-up, dusty pickup truck I didn't recognize and a Cadillac with a dented front end. But I didn't see Kelsi's car. Or Sydney's. Even her snob-mobile would have been a relief at this point.

"No one's here," I murmured.

Sam glanced over at me as he shifted his Jeep into park and cut the motor. "Lacey, it's still early," he said. "Don't worry yet."

"What if no one shows?" I asked.

"Then you and I will have a great time bowling together in really ugly shoes."

We got out of the Jeep and walked into the bowling alley. I had never been there before. We'd never been big on bowling in my family. Come to think of it, we weren't big on much of anything anymore.

The entrance area was dimly lit, while bright fluorescent lights illuminated the wood-paneled lanes. There were only three people bowling: a man and a woman together at a lane toward the far end of the room, and, midway down, a man in a FedEx uniform.

"I bet he's on his lunch break," Sam whispered, elbowing me gently in the side. I giggled as the FedEx guy bowled a strike and jumped up and down a few times in apparent glee.

The deep ping of the balls hitting pins punctuated the background music piped from various old-looking speakers around the room. There was a counter near the door with lots of bowling shoes lined up behind it, and another counter farther down with a couple of beer and soda taps, a popcorn machine, and a little warmer rotating some decidedly stale-looking hot dogs. I decided I wasn't hungry.

"Let me introduce you to my aunt," Sam said, reaching for my hand. A dark-haired woman was walking out from a door near the concession area. "Donna!" Sam called. She squinted toward the doorway and grinned.

"Hey, kiddo!" she said. It sounded funny to hear Sam called kiddo. His aunt's enthusiasm was electric, though, and I could feel myself smiling at her even before she reached us. She was about five feet eight with cropped hair, a few freckles across the bridge of her nose, and clear green eyes that matched Sam's.

She reached us quickly and gave Sam a hug. Then she extended a hand to me. "You must be Lacey," she said. "Sam's told me about you."

I blushed, wondering what he'd said–and when. "Nice to meet you. Thanks for letting us use your bowling alley."

"Of course!" she said. She glanced around, then looked back at me. "Where is everybody?"

Sam answered before I could. "They should be here in a few minutes. And if they don't show up, Lacey and I will bowl."

Donna smiled at us again. "Sounds fun! Help yourselves to bowling shoes. Sam, you know the drill," she said. "Can I get you anything from the concession stand? A hot dog, maybe?"

"No thanks," Sam and I both chorused immediately. We exchanged glances and tried not to laugh. Donna looked bewildered.

"Okay, then," she said. "Have fun! I'll be back to check

on you guys in a bit. Sam, you know where everything is when your other friends show up." She kissed him on the cheek. "Nice to meet you, Lacey," she said before walking away.

"She seems nice," I said to Sam as we turned toward the wall of bowling shoes.

"She's the best. She and my uncle are a ton of fun. Our family Trivial Pursuit matches are pretty fierce."

I suddenly wished that I had an aunt like that. Or another family member–any family member–who wasn't full of sympathetic looks. My uncle Paul and his wife, Sherry, came around from time to time, but Aunt Sherry was always casting sad glances my way, and Uncle Paul didn't seem to know how to talk to any of us anymore.

Sam led me over to the shoes and asked me for my size. A moment later, he pulled out a pair of pink and white shoes that were slightly scuffed at the toes. They were pretty silly-looking.

"Trust me," Sam said, reading my expression, "no one looks good in bowling shoes."

Just then, the front door opened, pouring a large sliver of bright sunshine into the bowling alley. I was relieved to see Kelsi and Mindy standing there, blinking into the darkness.

As Sam was helping Kelsi and Mindy pick out bowling shoes, Cody arrived, eyes downcast. As the five of us were heading toward the lanes, the door opened again, and Logan walked in, tailed a few steps behind by a sullen-looking Sydney.

Relief washed over me again, along with an unfamiliar

sense of gratitude for my brother, who didn't look at me as he walked quickly toward the shoe counter.

"Hey, man," Sam said to my brother as he walked over to the shoe counter. "Hey, Syd."

They both nodded, but neither of them said anything. Typical. Too cool to talk to anyone. But, I had to give Logan credit for being here. And, I supposed, I had to grudgingly give Sydney a little credit too, even if she didn't belong here. But clearly, she and Logan were a package deal.

After everyone was fitted, we headed to the lanes and picked two adjoining ones on the right. Donna came over and asked us if we wanted anything from the snack bar. Logan ordered two hot dogs. Sam and I shared amused looks, but neither of us said anything. I liked that we were on the inside of a private joke. The hot dogs arrived a few minutes later, along with a hot pretzel for Cody and three Cokes for the girls. I tried not to giggle as my brother gazed in horror at the shriveled-looking meat like it was something from another planet. It was even funnier when, unaware that he was being watched, he shrugged and bit into a hot dog anyway.

Sam, Kelsi, and I were in one lane, and Mindy, Cody, Sydney, and Logan took the lane beside us.

Neither Kelsi nor I had bowled much before, so Sam took a few minutes to patiently explain technique. He showed us how to grip the ball, how to take steps forward to support our weight, and how to aim for the center pin by angling the ball in slightly from the side. He demonstrated three different styles for us and got strikes each time.

On Kelsi's first turn, she knocked over three pins with

the first ball and another three pins with the second. Sam grinned and told her she was an excellent student. She blushed and sat down. I glanced at the lane next to us, where Logan and Sydney had each knocked over eight pins, and I wondered how my brother was so good at this. Maybe I would be too.

I stood up, took a deep breath, and put my fingers into the purple, glittery ball I had picked out. I tested its weight and hesitantly carried it toward the lane. I took a deep breath, moved my arm back like Sam had shown me, and then took a step forward as I moved my arm forward and released the ball.

It dropped into the gutter almost immediately.

I groaned as I watched it make its way down the edge of the lane.

"Nice gutter ball, Lacey," Sydney piped up, laughing.

Sam rolled his eyes. "It took me *forever* to learn to bowl," he told me. "Here." He got up and touched my arm lightly. "I'll show you."

I picked up my ball and we walked to the lane. "Put your arm back," Sam said.

I grasped the ball tightly and did what he said, stepping back with my left foot, like Sam had showed me. I was just about to ask him what to do next when I felt his warmth right behind me.

"Like this," he said softly, his breath grazing my ear as my cheeks flamed. He was so close that I could feel him, yet not close enough to be touching my back. Every single hair on my body was standing on end. He placed his right hand over mine, and I was so electrified by his touch that I nearly dropped the ball. Thankfully, I didn't.

"Okay, now," he said. "Let's do this slowly once to practice. Don't let go."

I knew he was talking about the bowling ball, but for a second, I wanted to tell him not to worry, that I would never let go. I glanced around and realized that everyone was watching us.

Slowly, with his right hand resting on mine and his left hand gently clasping my left hand, Sam guided my right arm forward, urging me, "Step forward with your left foot, like I showed you." He took the step with me, his much longer left leg shadowing my leg and his arm guiding mine forward.

"Just like that," he said in my ear. Then he cleared his throat loudly, glanced around, and stepped away, as if he'd just noticed that everyone was staring. "Um, nice job, Lacey," he said. "You're a natural. Now let's try it for real."

I knew my face was on fire. I glanced around and quickly returned my attention to the ball and the lane in front of me. I closed my eyes for a minute and tried to center myself. Repeating Sam's words in my head, I stepped back, then stepped forward, slowly swinging my right arm in one fluid motion.

I watched as the ball rolled slowly down the lane. It seemed to take forever, but this time, it didn't roll toward the gutter. In fact, it went straight down the middle. At the last second, it veered to the right and hit near the center. It knocked over seven pins!

I leapt up, ecstatic. I knew it wasn't exactly a strike, but it felt pretty good to me.

I wanted to see if everyone had noticed, but before I even had a chance to look around, Sam put his arms around me. And then, in front of everyone, he kissed me like it was the most normal thing in the world.

• • •

Two hours later, we had bowled two games, and I had gotten a little bit better. I even knocked over all ten pins on two tries. Still, I was by far the worst bowler in the group. I didn't care. What I cared about was that we *were* a group. All of us, who had nothing in common except for the biggest thing, had talked and laughed and had fun.

After we had changed back into our street shoes, we all thanked Donna and walked outside. The sun had gone down, and there were just a few remaining streaks of light in the sky to the west, the last remnants of the day. With the sunshine gone, a chill had set in, and none of us were dressed warmly enough. I shivered as we stood in the parking lot, looking at one another.

"That was fun," Cody said.

"Yeah," Mindy agreed.

"It *was* fun," Kelsi said after a minute. "But we didn't really talk about anything."

She was right. It just hadn't seemed like the time or the place to bring up sad stuff when, for once, we were having fun without thinking about it.

"Maybe we didn't need to," Cody said. "Maybe it's cool to hang out with each other sometimes and not have to talk about it."

"Yeah," Kelsi said. "All you guys want me to do is be myself. It's kind of nice."

After exchanging goodbyes and saying we'd see one another in school tomorrow, we started drifting toward our cars.

"Need a ride?" Sam asked, putting his hand lightly on my shoulder.

Sydney, seeing this and apparently deciding that she couldn't bear for someone else to be happy for a millisecond, jumped in. "I'll drive her home. I'm going there anyhow. Obviously."

Sam and I exchanged glances, and I shrugged.

"Okay," Sam said. I'd been kind of hoping he'd insist on driving me. He kissed my cheek and walked over to his Jeep. I watched him go, feeling a lot warmer than I should have in the evening air.

"Let's go," Sydney said, clapping her hands together. "It's cold out here."

I followed her and Logan to her car and climbed into the back. Sydney started the engine, and as we sat there for a minute to let it warm up, she and Logan whispered something to each other. I ignored them. Finally, Sydney pulled out of the lot.

"So," she said, glancing at me in the rearview mirror, "what's up with you and Sam?"

I knew it was coming. I took a deep breath. "We're going

out, I guess," I said. The words tasted sweet in my mouth. "But then again, you knew that," I heard myself add.

"What are you talking about?"

"Haven't you been gossiping about it all day?" I asked her.

Sydney huffed indignantly. "I don't gossip," she said. "How dare you accuse me of that?"

I laughed. "Right."

Sydney nudged my brother. "Lacey, I don't want to burst your bubble or anything, but it can't last, you know."

"What?" I looked at her face in the rearview mirror. I had no idea what she was talking about.

"I mean, it's just not a logical match," she said.

"What on earth do you mean?" I asked.

"Well," Sydney said slowly, like she was talking to a child, "you have to admit, it's not like you have anything in common. Other than your dead fathers."

The way Sydney said the words sliced into me.

"You barely know him," I said after a minute. "How could you possibly say that?"

"Think about it," she continued. "You're brainy. He's hot. And you're up against Summer Andrews. I mean, do you really think he's going to choose you over her in the long term?"

I had just opened my mouth to reply when my brother spoke up. "Syd, leave her alone."

Dead silence. I was as taken aback as Sydney was. Logan never came to my defense. Not anymore. And certainly not against Sydney.

Sydney sputtered for a second. I knew she was flailing for a retort.

Logan sighed again. "We'll talk about it later, Sydney," he said with more finality than I'd ever heard in his voice.

"But–"

"Not now," Logan said. Then he turned and looked out the window, effectively ending the conversation.

I turned and looked out the window too, biting my lip and trying not to smile. I didn't know what had just happened, but somehow, Logan seemed to be back on my side, even if only a little bit.

• • •

Even though I knew she was just being a jerk, I couldn't shake Sydney's words. They had wormed their way into my brain, making me wonder if I was being naïve to believe that what Sam and I had was real. Maybe Sydney was right. I didn't want to think that the only reason Sam liked me was because he saw a reflection of his own pain. But maybe that was all it was.

Mom actually made it home for dinner that night, so the four of us sat down to a meal that she had "cooked"–spaghetti with sauce out of a jar and a bagged salad.

"This is nice," Mom said as we chewed in silence. Tanner slurped a noodle noisily and looked up, the faintest trace of a smile on his face. "You know, we hardly ever eat together anymore."

"Maybe it's because you're never home," Logan said.

Mom sighed heavily. "Logan, someone has to support

this family. You know I'd love to spend more time with you. It just isn't able to work out that way right now."

Logan was silent for so long that I thought he was going to let it go. And for a moment, I was very relieved. Dinners together were so rare that I didn't want this one to be spoiled by a fight. But then Logan said slowly, "That's bullshit."

Mom flinched, like she'd been struck. "What did you say?"

"I said it's bullshit," Logan said.

Tanner and I exchanged glances. "Logan," I said as my mom gaped at him. "I really don't think–"

"Shut up, Lacey," he cut me off. "I'm so sick and tired of everyone tiptoeing around the truth."

"Young man," my mother began. But her voice was shaky and lacked conviction.

"Don't 'young man' me," my brother snapped. "You don't have the right anymore."

"I'm your mother," she said.

Logan shook his head. "My mother disappeared last November."

I hated the way he was hurting my mom, but despite myself, I agreed with him. I wanted to defend her, but I couldn't. I held my breath.

"You know, you can't run from it, Mom," he said. "Dad's dead, okay? Dead, dead, dead."

"Logan!" she exclaimed. There were tears welling in her eyes.

"You keep acting like if you just work enough, if you just avoid your family, if you go out and have fun and play tennis and keep your hair perfect and your clothes ironed, it will all go away," he went on. "But it won't. You're just lying to yourself. You can't make everything perfect, because it's not. Dad is dead, Mom. He *died.* I watched him, okay? I watched him die. You can't pretend."

My mom was crying and I felt a tightening in my own chest. There were tears in Tanner's eyes too, and he made a little choked sound before setting down his fork.

Logan wasn't done. "You don't even act like a mom anymore," he continued. "You remember what it used to be like? Huh? Do you? You used to ask us about school. You used to joke around. You used to be fun. You used to care. But now all you care about is forgetting. You think that's how Dad would want you to be?"

My mother was sobbing full force now, but Logan didn't seem to notice. His face was red, and his hands were clenched into fists, like he was waiting to defend himself against some unexpected attack.

"Logan," I began.

"And you!" he exclaimed, turning on me. "You think that by being Little Miss Perfect, you can fix everything," he accused. "Well, you're as stupid as she is!" He nodded in Mom's direction. "You don't even have a clue. You think you're so much better than me just because you make straight As and you take care of everyone and you never cry. But you know what? That's really screwed up."

"What?" I choked out.

"You're such a phony," he spat.

"Shut up," I whispered. "You don't know what you're talking about."

"Yeah, well, what are you going to tell me?" he mocked. "I mean, you seem to have all the answers, right?"

"I never said I had all the answers."

Logan snorted. "You didn't have to." He pulled his napkin off his lap, balled it up, and tossed it onto the table. "Thanks for the great dinner. This has been fun."

He got up and strode away without another word. We all watched him go, shocked into silence. Then we all looked at one another.

Tanner was the first to move. As he stood up from the table, he knocked his milk glass over with his elbow. It crashed onto the floor, shattering into a hundred little pieces. His eyes filled. "Sorry," he whispered.

"It's okay, honey," my mom said, her voice pinched. "I'll take care of it." Tanner darted out of the room. I could hear his footsteps on the stairs, then the slamming of his bedroom door.

Silence settled over us. My mother and I looked at each other, then down at the floor, where the shards of shattered glass reflected the light.

"We'd better clean that up," my mother said. But she didn't move. She just kept staring at the glass, like she was wondering whether it would really be possible to ever pick up all the pieces.

chapter 17

I told Sam about the fight the next day, and he said that sometimes people don't think before they speak, and that Logan probably hadn't meant the things he said.

"But he did mean it," I said as we sat across from each other at McDonald's after school, sharing a large chocolate milk shake in alternate slurps. "And the thing was, he was right."

"About what?" Sam asked.

"About everything," I admitted. "I mean, all the things he said about my mom were the things I've been thinking. Maybe he was right about me, too."

"Or maybe Logan was just telling you the way he sees things," Sam said, "which doesn't necessarily make it right."

On Friday night, he and I went out with Brian and Jennica to the movies, and as we sat in the darkened theater, with our fingers intertwined, I thought how nice it was not to feel like a third wheel for once. I hated that I needed another person to make me feel like I belonged. But if I had to have someone at my side to help me fit, I was glad it was Sam.

On Saturday, Sam had practice for a soccer league he'd joined in town. He asked me if I wanted to come sit in the park with a few of the other girlfriends while he kicked the ball around with the guys, and I agreed instantly. It wasn't that I wanted to spend every waking second with him or anything. It was that I was avoiding my house. It was even more silent than usual, which was weird, because Mom was actually home. Logan's words had evidently penetrated; she had come home every night before seven, and she canceled her Saturday tennis plans to catch up on some housework. That was a first.

Sunday, Jennica and I went to the mall and then got sundaes at Brigham's. We talked about guys, and for the first time in ages, I had something to contribute. I told her what Sydney had said earlier in the week, and she reassured me that Sydney was just jealous and mean. I knew this, but even with Jennica's words of comfort, I still couldn't shake the feeling that something was wrong.

Sam didn't call on Sunday night, which was weird, because he had started calling me every night so that we could wish each other sweet dreams. But I tried not to read into it; he was probably just busy.

On Monday morning, though, he wasn't in first period. As the final bell rang, and his seat remained ominously empty, a funny feeling settled over me.

"Where is he?" Jennica mouthed as she glanced at Sam's seat, then at my confused face. Mrs. Bost had already started class and was babbling something about vectors, but I couldn't seem to tune in.

"I don't know," I mouthed back.

My phone vibrated a moment later, and I snuck a look. Jennica had texted im sure theres an explanation. I nodded and looked away, trying to focus on Mrs. Bost. But I had a feeling that something was wrong.

At lunchtime, I snuck outside to call Sam, but his voice mail picked up on the first ring. We weren't supposed to talk on our cells at school, but I left him a quick message asking him to call me when he could.

He wasn't in sixth period either, and he hadn't called back. I tried him again as I was getting my books out of my locker after school, but his phone still went straight to voice mail. I was so busy agonizing over the reasons behind his absence that I didn't even notice Cody approach until he was right in front of me.

"Hey," he said. His hands were jammed in his pockets, and he looked nervous.

I stopped at my locker and looked at him. "Hey."

"So, um," he began. He coughed and looked down. "Are we on for tomorrow?"

"Tomorrow?" I asked.

"Well, it's Tuesday, isn't it?" he said. "Are we still having a meeting?"

"Yeah," I said, feeling good for the first time today. "What do you want to do?"

Cody shrugged. "I dunno. I'm supposed to watch my sister, Sarah, tomorrow afternoon. She's ten. Think we could go somewhere where I could bring her?"

I nodded. "Sure. I'll talk to everybody."

By that evening, I had gotten in touch with Kelsi and Mindy and we had agreed to meet at the ice rink at Plymouth Center.

I told Logan, who reluctantly agreed to try to come, even though we were barely talking to each other, and I asked my mom if I could take Tanner, too, since Cody's sister was about his age. I thought it might be good for my little brother.

"Whatever you want," my mom said with a shrug. I wasn't even one hundred percent sure she heard me.

That evening, I called Sam once more and left another message. And then, because I didn't know whether I should be hurt or worried, I went onto our local newspaper's Web site to check for traffic accidents. There hadn't been anything serious enough to be covered. Sam wasn't lying by the side of the road somewhere. Just to be sure, I searched the site for his name, but nothing came up.

I swallowed my pride and sent Sam an e-mail, telling him that the group was meeting the next day at four at the ice rink if he wanted to come.

The next morning, I checked my e-mail as soon as I got up, but there was no reply from Sam. He wasn't in school all day either. I couldn't figure out what was wrong or why he couldn't call me back. Why was he avoiding me?

After school, Sydney drove me and Logan home, and we picked up Tanner to take him to the ice rink. Cody, Kelsi, and Mindy were already waiting for us when we got there. Cody's little sister Sarah turned out to be a tiny girl with long, frizzy hair. She talked a mile a minute and sounded like a miniature adult.

"Hi, you must be Lacey," she began rapid-fire, without taking a breath. "I'm Sarah and my brother told me about you and I love ice skating, so he thought I'd want to come along, and my dad died, but it's not like we have to just talk about that, because there are lots of other interesting things we can talk about too, like ice skating or school or sports or something, and is that your brother over there?"

She finally paused for breath and cocked her head inquisitively.

I followed her eyes to Tanner, who was hanging back from the crowd. He had brought his own knee pads and helmet and didn't seem the slightest bit worried about appearing dorky. The only thing I'd been able to get out of him when I asked why he'd come prepared was, "Dad always told me better safe than sorry."

I nodded at Sarah. "Yeah, his name's Tanner," I said. "He doesn't talk much, though."

She nodded wisely. "Some kids don't talk much after their parents have died," she said. "But I've always talked, and when my dad died, I just started talking some more, and now I talk all the time, and I think it drives my brother and my mom crazy, but I can't really help it, you know, and maybe if I talk enough to your brother, maybe he'll talk back to me, and we can be friends, even though he's a year older than me, but we go to the same school. I see him on the playground at lunch and he's usually by himself, even though kids like him, but he's really quiet, and maybe we can hang out sometime."

I blinked at Sarah a few times, trying to keep up with the words pouring out of her mouth. "Um, yeah," I said. "That sounds good." I glanced over at Tanner, who was carefully pulling on his bright blue knee pads. I felt sad for him. I looked back at Sarah. "I think he could use a friend."

I expected another torrent of words, but instead she just said, "Me too."

I watched as Sarah went over to Tanner and said something to him. He looked at her blankly, then nodded. She launched into another long-winded sentence, which I couldn't hear, and when she finally paused for breath, I watched as Tanner searched her face for what felt like an eternity and then finally broke into a hesitant grin. I was startled; I hadn't seen him smile in a while.

Feeling relieved, I went to pick up skates for Tanner and me at the counter.

Ten minutes later, all of us were out on the ice.

"Where's Sam?" Kelsi asked as we inched along, trying to get our balance.

"I don't know," I said.

"You told him about the meeting?" Mindy asked in a soft voice.

"Yeah," I said. "I mean, I left him a message. He hasn't called back."

I looked up, expecting to see judgment or pity on their faces. After all, they knew Sam and I were going out, and now he wasn't even replying to me. But they only looked concerned. "Well, it's not really the same without all of us here," Kelsi said. "When you talk to him, tell him we missed him today, okay?"

Kelsi and Mindy partnered up after a few minutes, and, holding each other's hands and giggling, they picked their way around the rink. I stopped and just watched them. Before I'd put this group together, they'd hardly known each other. And here they were, laughing on a Tuesday afternoon, just weeks after Kelsi's mom had died, when she might otherwise have been at home, wallowing in grief.

Logan and Sydney made their way a little more quickly. It looked like Sydney was leading Logan, who was a bit slower, dragging him by the hand and chiding him when he couldn't keep up. Still, he appeared content.

Cody was off in his own world, whizzing across the ice like he was on the Olympic speed skating team. Each time he passed, his cheeks were flushed, and his eyes were focused straight ahead. I wondered if he was doing more than exercising; it looked like he might have been getting something out of his system.

I skated alone, and it gave me time to think about Sam–and about my dad. The anniversary of the accident was fast approaching, and it seemed like I should be in a different place. I knew that what I had done with setting up this club was good; it seemed to be helping. And I knew that was something I had to do: help other people come to terms with a parent's death, like I had. But still, the emptiness loomed inside of me, big and cold. I'd never felt so lonely.

While the rink was cleared temporarily for the ice to be Zambonied, I sat down and closed my eyes. No one was paying attention to me. Kelsi and Mindy were talking about some sophomore guy Mindy liked. Logan and Sydney were cooing at each other in the corner–I was afraid they were going to start making out any minute. Cody had disappeared to the other side of the rink, where he apparently knew three girls in skating outfits.

And for the first time in ages, I heard Tanner's voice loud and clear for more than a few words at a stretch as he talked to Sarah.

"What happened?" I heard him ask. I strained to hear, feeling a little bad that I was eavesdropping.

"My dad was in the military, in Iraq, you know, which is really far away, and we couldn't see him very often because his job was dangerous and he had to be gone for a long time," Sarah was saying, speaking at the speed of light. I glanced over and was surprised to see my little brother staring at her with rapt interest. "I was always scared that something would happen to my dad, because I heard about Army guys getting hurt, and he always told me not to worry because he'd be here forever, so I tried not to worry. But he was supposed to come home on March sixteenth, and it was March ninth, and I was really excited and I was making him a big picture of our house so he could see what everything looked like while he was gone, and I was outside doing the drawing, and two military men pulled up in the driveway."

"Military men?" Tanner repeated.

"Yeah, they were wearing really fancy uniforms with lots of ribbons and stuff, and I think they were really important," Sarah babbled on. "And they called me 'little girl,' even though I'm not that little, and they looked really serious, and they asked if my mom was home, and I said yeah, and I asked what they wanted, and they wouldn't tell me, but I had a bad feeling about it, so I ran and got my mom, and they whispered something to her and then she just started crying. I didn't know what to do because I'd never seen her cry before, and she fell down on the driveway, and they didn't know what to do either; they just stood there looking down at her and saying it would be okay, and they could help her."

"Oh," Tanner said softly.

Sarah went on. "I went and got Cody, I don't even remember what I said, but I think I was screaming really loud, and he came out of the house and bent over and hugged my mom, and he asked the military men what was wrong, and they told him that my dad had died, I heard them tell him that, and then he started crying too, and I started screaming again, because I didn't know what else to do, and I wanted to ask them if my dad was in heaven, and I wanted to ask my mom that too, but she was crying, and the military men looked mean, and I didn't know what they'd say, and besides, they were treating me like a baby."

Tanner was quiet for a minute, and my heart sank for Sarah. She had opened up to him the way I had to Sam, and my brother wasn't going to answer her, simply because he couldn't.

But then, my brother spoke, which surprised me so much that I nearly fell over. "I believe in heaven," he said quietly. "I know your dad has to be there. Because he was doing the right thing when he died."

I heard Sarah sniffle a little. "You think?" she ventured.

I was afraid Tanner wouldn't answer. Then he said, "Yeah."

They sat there in silence for a moment, and when I was pretty sure that the conversation was finally over, I peeked my head around a chair to take a look at them. Perhaps Tanner, having spoken his entire word quota for the past three months, had gotten up and left, or spontaneously combusted from the mental exertion.

Instead, they were sitting side by side in companionable silence, staring out at the Zamboni making its slow loops around the rink, smoothing the surface of the roughed-up ice. I waited for Sarah to say something more–after all, she seemed to be overflowing with words–but she didn't seem to have anything else to say. After a minute, she put her head on my brother's shoulder. He paused and then put an arm around her shoulders. From the back, they looked like miniature adults. I could hardly believe it was my little brother, the one who hid in his room, watching TV and obsessing over animals.

Maybe, I thought, he was better off than I'd given him credit for. Maybe he'd get better with or without my help and concern. Maybe I was wasting my time fearing for his mental health.

Maybe he didn't need me at all.

chapter 18

By Friday, Sam still hadn't shown up at school. He wasn't calling me back either, and I was really worried. There was still a part of me that was scared it had to do with me, but I reassured myself that no one in his right mind would skip school for five days because of a girl. I'd e-mailed him twice more, but I'd gotten no reply. I was starting to feel like a stalker.

After school, I caught a ride with Jennica and asked if she'd mind dropping me off at Lucky Strikes. "Sure, but I can't stay and drive you home," she said. "Anne has dance practice, and I have to take her. My mom's having a spa day, so I'm stuck babysitting." She rolled her eyes for emphasis. "Why are you going there anyhow?"

"Just meeting the group," I lied. I knew I should tell her that I was looking for Sam, but I didn't want to feel any more pathetic than I already did.

Five minutes later, I was standing in front of Lucky Strikes, staring at the door and wondering if this was stupid. I took a deep breath and walked in.

It took a moment for my eyes to adjust to the darkness inside the alley, but when they did, I spotted Donna seated behind the cash register, reading a paperback James Patterson novel. She was so absorbed in the book that she didn't even look up until I was standing right in front of her. I had to clear my throat to get her attention.

"Oh, Lacey!" she exclaimed. She peered at me. "Hi! How are you?"

I shrugged, suddenly feeling embarrassed to be there.

"I'm okay," I said. "Um, I was just wondering if Sam is around."

I felt stupid the moment the words were out of my mouth.

Donna looked confused. "Sam?" she said. "No, Lacey. He's at the hospital."

My heart caught in my throat. "The hospital?" I croaked. "What happened? Is he okay?"

Guilt flooded through me.

Donna was looking at me more closely now. "You don't know?" she asked.

"Know what?" I demanded. I felt like I was on the verge of panicking.

She studied me while my heart pounded double time. It looked like she was trying to decide whether to tell me or not.

"Please, just tell me if Sam's okay," I pleaded. I didn't think I could handle it if something happened to someone else I cared about. In an instant, all the awful things that could have happened to Sam flashed through my head. And for some reason, my mind got immediately stuck on Sam in a car crash. A cold chill ran through me.

"Sam's fine," she said.

Relief flooded through me, followed quickly by confusion. "Why's he at the hospital, then?"

She put down her book. "It's his dad, Lacey."

"His dad?" I repeated. What was she talking about? Hadn't he died months ago?

"He woke up," Donna said softly.

My jaw dropped. "Woke up? But . . . he's dead."

Now it was Donna's turn to look confused. "Dead?" she repeated. "Where did you get that idea?"

A feeling began to creep through my veins like ice. Every conversation I'd ever had with Sam began to replay itself in my mind. Is this what he had wanted to tell me? But even if it was, how could he let me go on believing something so huge when it had been a lie all along?

"He's not dead?" I whispered. Donna shook her head. "But Sam said he had a stroke."

Donna nodded. "He did. He's been in a coma since July. They moved him to Plymouth Regional Hospital in September. That's why Sam and his mom moved here."

I stared at her in disbelief. She must have thought I was

totally crazy, but I couldn't help repeating, "You're telling me he's alive?"

"Yes. And he woke up on Sunday night. The doctors are calling it a miracle. Sam and Joey and their mom have been at his bedside since then."

I stared at her. I couldn't form words. I couldn't think of anything to say.

"Lacey?" she asked. Her face radiated concern. "Are you all right, honey?"

"Um" was all I could manage. I shook my head. "I'm sorry. Thank you."

I felt like the walls were closing in on me. I slowly backed away from her and out of the bowling alley. It wasn't until I was outside, in the crisp fall afternoon air, that I realized I didn't have a ride home. Numbly, feeling like the wind had been knocked out of me and I couldn't quite catch my breath, I began walking toward my house.

• • •

By the time I walked up my own driveway I didn't feel any better. I knew I should be happy for Sam that he'd gotten his father back. Wouldn't I have given anything in the world to hear the same kind of news about my dad? But the fact was, I never would hear that news; my father was gone for good.

I'd believed the same about Sam's dad. Sam had *made* me believe the same about his dad. And that's why I'd trusted him with my feelings, my secrets. That's why I'd believed, in the very depth of my soul, that he understood me. But the truth was, he didn't know any more about how I felt than Jennica or Dr. Schiff or any of the kids at school who lived in their perfect homes with their perfectly complete families.

I began to replay in my head every conversation I'd ever had with Sam. He'd never directly lied, I couldn't actually remember the words "My dad died" coming out of his mouth. But from the day he showed up at our first meeting, saying that he'd lost his dad, I had trusted him and had assumed that he'd meant his dad was no longer alive. Why would I think anything different? But just because he hadn't blatantly lied didn't make the betrayal any less serious. He knew what he'd led us to believe. He knew what he'd led *me* to believe. And it hadn't mattered.

Why had he done it? Had he been that desperate to fit in with us? Sam didn't seem to care about being popular, and it wasn't even like we were a popular group. Besides, who in their right minds would fake a parental death to become part of a clique? No, it went deeper than that. I had no doubt that losing your dad to a coma was really hard. And I was sure that to some extent, Sam *had* understood us and identified with us. But the fundamental difference was that *his dad had woken up.* Mindy, Kelsi, Cody, Logan, and I would never have that experience. We couldn't. And for Sam to think it was okay to trick us in this way made me feel sick.

The sky darkened as I walked home, and as I reached my front door, the first fat raindrops of an approaching storm began to fall, splashing on the driveway and pinging off the roof of the house. I put my key in the lock and closed my eyes before turning it, steadying myself.

I would never let anyone in again. I couldn't trust anyone. The world around me had crumbled, and once again, it was still me, only me, standing there on my own.

I should have known better.

• • •

Mom was home from work early again, standing in the kitchen and absentmindedly beating something in a big bowl, when I walked in.

She smiled. "Hi, honey."

I raised a hand to wave without a word. I didn't feel like talking to her. Or anyone else. Sam's betrayal had been the final straw.

"Sam called," Mom said. She wiped her hands on her apron and crossed over to the notepad that we kept by the kitchen phone. "He left a number and an extension and asked that you call him back as soon as possible. He said he tried your cell, but it went straight to voice mail."

I gazed at her in disbelief. *Now* he had called? After I'd been trying to reach him all week? Donna had probably called him and told him what had happened.

"Lacey?" Mom asked. "Don't you want the number?"

I glanced at the pad of paper and then back at her. "No."

She shrugged. "Well. I'm just about to put a soufflé in the oven," she said, turning away from me and returning to the hand beater. "I thought I'd try something new for dinner."

"Really?" I asked, surprised. Mom used to love to cook–she subscribed to *Bon Appétit* and *Food & Wine* and a few other cooking magazines–and before the accident, she would try something new and exotic at least once a week.

"Yeah," she said. "I think I need to stop."

"Stop what?" I asked.

She looked down at the bowl. "Stop wallowing. Logan was right the other day."

The rain had started to fall harder now, and the fat droplets had given way to an insistent waterfall that made it look fuzzy and almost dreamlike outside.

"I've been awful," she added, gazing out the kitchen window. "I've really failed you kids."

"No, you haven't," I said. It felt like the right thing to say, but I realized, after the words were out of my mouth, that I meant it.

"Yes, I have," she said. She took a deep breath and let it out slowly. "It's been almost a year, Lacey. A year of our lives that I've lost. Your father wouldn't have wanted it this way."

"I think he would have understood, Mom."

"Understood what?"

"Understood that we all needed to figure out things in our own time."

Mom blinked a few times. "Maybe it's time to start living again."

As I walked slowly out of the kitchen, I thought about the last thing she had said. At least we *had* the luxury to start living again. Logan and Tanner and Mom and I, Sam and his mom, even Sam's dad, could start over at any time. It made me even sadder to think about it in those terms.

Because it seemed unfair, like a betrayal of Dad, to be able to just reinvent ourselves any day, didn't it? We'd all have a thousand–a million–second chances.

Dad wouldn't even have one.

• • •

When I checked my e-mail before going to bed that night, there was one new message waiting for me in my in-box. It was from Sam.

Lacey,

I don't even know how to begin. I know you feel like I lied to you. And I don't blame you. But I didn't do it on purpose. I heard about the group you were starting, and I didn't know until the end of the first meeting that it was only for people whose parents had actually died. But by that time, I felt so much better just being there. I know you might not understand, but it felt like my dad had died, just like yours. He wasn't supposed to wake up, ever, and in a way, I felt sometimes like it would have been better if he did just die, because then we could at least have a funeral and say a real goodbye and everything.

I was with my dad when he had the stroke. The doctors said he would never regain consciousness. And then, Sunday night, we got a call from the hospital. The nurse on duty had noticed the call light from his room was on. She went in to check on him, figuring it was a mistake, and he was sitting up in bed, looking confused. He didn't know where he was. They called the doc and then they called us. My mom hasn't wanted to leave his side since then. We've been sleeping at the hospital. She keeps saying it's our second chance.

I know you're mad at me. I tried to tell you, but I guess I didn't try hard enough. I was scared about how you'd react. I thought you wouldn't believe anymore that I knew how you felt. But I do. I'm sorry. I can't even tell you how sorry I am. But I never meant to hurt you. And it doesn't take away the fact that I do understand you. Please call me.

Sam

I read the e-mail three times before closing the screen. My finger hovered over the Delete key, but finally, I hit Save instead.

I understood what he was saying. But that didn't make his actions easier to understand. Or to forgive.

chapter 19

I tried to talk to Dr. Schiff about Sam on Saturday during my half-hour session with her. She told me I needed to stop holding other people to an unrealistic standard. I'd asked her what was so unrealistic about expecting someone to be honest. I called Jennica and filled her in on everything, and she was totally sympathetic. "I'm beginning to think that all guys are more trouble than they're worth," she told me. I wasn't sure I agreed with her, though. No matter how mad I was at Sam.

Tanner had Cody's sister, Sarah, over on Sunday. They watched TV and played video games, and I could hear them laughing. I felt a strange blend of relief, pride, and jealousy. Relief, because it meant there was hope for Tanner. Pride, because if I hadn't started the group that included Cody, Tanner wouldn't have met Sarah. And, embarrassingly, jealousy, because Tanner was learning how to cope while I seemed to be getting more and more lost by the day.

On Monday morning, I walked into trig class to find Sam waiting by my seat.

"Hey, Lacey," he said, like we were the only two people in the room.

"Hey," I mumbled, both wanting and not wanting to see him.

"Lacey," Sam said, putting his hand on mine.

I bit my lower lip and moved my hand away. "I don't want to talk to you."

"Look, I'm sorry," he said. "I really am. Did you get my e-mail?"

"Yeah," I said. I paused. "And I'm glad your dad woke up." I really was, and I wanted him to know that.

"Thanks," he said. "And Lacey, for what it's worth, I'm sorry."

"You lied to us," I whispered. "You lied to *me*."

"I never lied," he said, shaking his head. "I just–I just didn't correct the misunderstanding."

• • •

After school I walked home by myself. I didn't know where Logan was, and Jennica had to stay after school to work on a history group project.

The sun was low in the sky. The days were getting shorter and the nights longer, but that was okay; I liked the darkness. It was only four in the afternoon, but the first colors of sunset were starting to gather on the horizon.

I was so lost in thought five minutes later that it barely registered when a vehicle slowed beside me.

"Lacey?"

It was Sam in his Cherokee, his window rolled down. "Lacey, get in," he said. "It's cold out."

I shook my head, not stopping. "I'm fine." But Sam kept inching his Jeep along.

"I'll follow you the whole way home if you want," Sam said. "But wouldn't it be easier to just get in? It's not getting any warmer."

I snorted and quickened my pace. "I like to walk."

But Sam was right. I only had a denim jacket on, and the cold was starting to seep into my bones. It was another fifteen minutes home. I'd be fine, but the heated interior of a car was admittedly tempting.

"Please, Lacey? Just give me a chance to talk to you for five minutes."

I hesitated, watching my warm breath crystallize into little white clouds. Finally, I got in.

"Thanks," Sam said. He glanced in the rearview mirror as I buckled my seat belt. Then he pulled slowly away from the curb.

We didn't say anything for a little while. Then Sam said, "Look, Lacey. I'm sorry."

I shrugged and looked out the window. The oranges

and pinks to the west were inching farther up the sky as the horizon began to tug the curtain down on the day.

"I'm glad for you," I said. "I'm glad your dad is fine."

"No you're not," Sam said. His words sliced into me, and I turned to look at him.

"I *am,*" I said. "Really. I would give anything in the world to have my dad back. And I'm glad that's happening to you. But the thing is, you tricked me. You made me feel like you understood me."

"I *do* understand."

My breath felt heavy, and the air around me seemed suddenly in short supply. I gazed at the sky again and thought about what Sam had said about rainbows. It had all been just words. "You *can't* understand!" I said. My eyes felt dry, and I blinked a few times, trying to get the burning sensation to go away. "Your dad is alive, Sam! You have another chance with him. You can talk to him and tell him about your day and tell him you love him. Even when he was in a coma, you could say all those things to him, and there was a chance he could hear you."

"Lacey, don't you think your dad can hear you too?" he asked.

I rolled my eyes. His words that night about rainbows and my dad looking over us just sounded ridiculous now. "No," I said. "And I think you're pretty much the last person who should be saying something like that to me."

We had pulled into my neighborhood. I was silent as Sam parked his Jeep alongside the curb in front of my house. I glanced at him and was surprised to see how wounded he looked. I suddenly felt a little bad.

"Is he doing okay?" I asked. "Your dad, I mean?"

Sam nodded. "It's hard to watch him," he said. "He can't move the right side of his face. He talks funny, and he can't remember a lot of words."

"But he's alive," I couldn't help but add.

"Yeah."

Then, before he had a chance to say anything else, I climbed out of the Jeep and slammed the door behind me. I could feel Sam watching me the whole way to the house. I had to stop myself from looking back at the street when I let myself in the front door.

• • •

That night, Sam sent an e-mail to everyone in the group.

> When I came to the first meeting, I didn't realize right away that it was supposed to only be for people whose parents had died. By the time I realized, I didn't know how to tell you guys. I felt really good around you; it feels weird to have a parent in a coma too, and we didn't think he was going to wake up, so I felt like I'd lost my dad too. I didn't mean to trick anyone, and I'm really sorry if anyone feels that way. You guys really helped me, and I would love to keep spending time with you if you'll have me.

Cody wrote back an e-mail, copied to the rest of us:

Glad your dad's okay. You don't have to apologize to us.

No one else responded—or if they did, they didn't CC everyone. I wondered how Cody could act so forgiving. Did Mindy and Kelsi feel the same way I did? Or was I the only one who was upset?

But the thing was, I was the one who had opened myself up.

I was the one who got hurt.

chapter 20

The next two weeks passed quickly. Sam was absent from school pretty often, and when he was there, I avoided him. Soon he stopped trying so hard to talk to me or to get me to forgive him. I think he knew it wasn't going to happen.

In English class, where he and I usually partnered up, he began working on projects with Matt Alexander, and I started working with Gillian Zucker. We had two Tuesday meetings of our group—one at McDonald's (where we all got Happy Meals and giggled our way through playing with the toys like little kids) and one at the ice rink again—

and I don't think I was the only one who felt Sam's absence.

Sunday, November fifteenth dawned gray and bleak, which seemed fitting. It was officially the anniversary. It had been an entire year. Today we'd begin a whole new year of days my father would never get to live, things he'd never get to see. But saying it, admitting it had been nearly a year already, was more difficult than it should have been.

It had been fifty-two Saturdays since I'd taken my sweet time in the bathroom and cheerfully headed out the door for the five-minute car ride that would change our lives. I felt tears prickle at the backs of my eyes as I lay in bed.

Despite myself, I went to the window to look for a rainbow, and I almost wanted to kick myself for believing there was even a chance one would be there. Not only did I not believe in stuff like that, but it would have been scientifically impossible, given the overcast skies. You needed sunshine for a rainbow, and I had the feeling there wouldn't be any today.

I looked at the sky anyhow, hoping that there would be some kind of sign that my dad was up there, watching. But still, nothing.

Then, something made me look down. My window overlooked the front yard and the street, and as I glanced at the grass, I noticed the strangest thing.

The lawn, which had been covered for the past few weeks in a growing blanket of orange, red, and yellow leaves, had been raked, and there was a big pile of leaves in the corner, almost exactly where my dad used to put the leaf pile.

For a fleeting instant, I was sure my dad had done it, that it was the sort of sign Sam had talked about, except that instead of painting a rainbow in the sky, my dad had done something much more personal.

Then I remembered. I had told Sam about the leaves, hadn't I? But he couldn't have done this. With as coldly as I'd been treating him, it was hard to believe that he would show up with a rake in the wee, cold hours of the morning and do something so incredibly touching.

I stared down from the window for a long time at the leaf pile. And while I looked, a little bit of the ice melted from around the outside of my heart.

• • •

Mom surprised us all by making light, fluffy blueberry pancakes for breakfast.

"I thought it would be a start to a tough day that your dad would appreciate," she said as she brought the platter to the table. Logan shuffled over to the fridge to grab the maple and blueberry syrups, and Tanner poured juice for all of us, sloshing a little over the side of Mom's glass.

"Sorry," he said.

She smiled at him. "No problem."

It was like we were in a time warp and had gone back to normal. Well, almost. Logan didn't look at all like himself; his eyes were bloodshot, his hair was a mess, and I could swear I could smell alcohol on him, although Mom seemed oblivious. Mom still looked vacant, but I knew she was trying. And Tanner, of course, was being his usual quiet self.

Or so I thought. After we'd downed our pancakes and Mom had stood up to start clearing the table, he suddenly said, "Knock, knock."

We all looked at him. Logan and I exchanged glances. Mom stopped in her tracks.

"What?" I asked, sure that I must have heard him wrong.

"Knock, knock," Tanner repeated.

We hadn't heard a joke come out of Tanner's mouth in a year. "Um, who's there?" I asked.

"Little old lady," he said.

"Little old lady who?" my mom asked, coming back to the table.

Tanner smiled at her and then at Logan and me. "I didn't know you could yodel, Mom."

It was a stupid joke, really, the kind that we only would have laughed at a year ago to be polite. But hearing Tanner tell it today, after a year of barely hearing his voice, never mind his humor, unleashed something in all of us.

Mom started laughing first, in high, tinkling tones that I hadn't heard in so long I had almost forgotten what they sounded like. Logan joined in next with an amused chuckle. Before I knew it, I was laughing too.

"I've been saving that one for today," Tanner said. "I think Dad would have liked it."

The words brought the laughter to a halt. Finally, Mom broke the silence. "Yes, Tanner," she said. "I know he would have."

And in that moment, sitting around the kitchen table with my mom and two brothers I felt like maybe, just maybe, our dad was with us after all.

• • •

Logan disappeared after breakfast with promises that he'd meet us back at the house by two to go to the cemetery, a trip I was dreading. I'd managed to avoid it for an entire year, but I knew I had to go. I had to do it. For my mom, for Tanner, and, I guess, for myself. After I took a shower and got dressed, I knocked on Tanner's door.

"Want to go out and jump in the leaf pile in the yard?" I asked.

He followed me outside. We spent the next hour jumping around together, like we used to when we were younger. We threw handfuls of leaves at each other, made leaf angels in the yard by lying on our backs and spreading our arms, and dove into the pile again and again, breathing in the familiar, slightly musty smell of autumn all around us.

We laughed like we used to when our dad would dive in with us, and as I grabbed my little brother for a tickle attack, like Dad used to do to me, I looked up at the gray sky once again, foolishly half expecting a rainbow. Instead there were just low, dense clouds and the promise of rain. The leaves, I knew, would get wet and soggy and would disperse around the yard again when the sky opened up. But for now, they were perfect, and when I closed my eyes, I could almost believe that it was like before, a crisp fall day when everything in the world was right.

• • •

Logan didn't come home.

As we waited for him at the kitchen table, my mom got more and more mad.

"Maybe he's just running late," she said at 2:10.

"He must be on his way," she said at 2:20 when she called his cell phone and it went straight to voice mail.

"What could they be doing?" she demanded at 2:30 when she called Sydney's phone and got her voice mail too.

"Fine, he can meet us there," she huffed at 2:45 when Logan still hadn't appeared.

So Mom, Tanner, and I climbed into the car and headed to the cemetery.

After we parked, Mom led us up the little hill to Dad's grave, as easily as if she had a map of the place imprinted on her mind. I supposed maybe she did.

Dad's gravestone was a thick slab of dark gray marble, and as we walked up to it, the words imprinted on it burned into me.

PETER MANN

BELOVED FATHER, HUSBAND, AND SON

A single ray of sunshine poked through the gloomy mass of clouds as we stood in silence, looking at Dad's grave. I had no idea how to act. Was I supposed to kneel and say a prayer? Or look up at the sky and try to talk to him? Was I supposed to touch the gravestone or the flowers that seemed to have no right to be alive while my father lay dead?

My mom started crying. Tanner stood beside her, holding her hand, his head leaning against her arm.

"Lacey," she said, turning toward me.

I swallowed hard and wondered what was wrong with me that I wasn't crying too. I joined them, putting my arm around Mom. She pulled me into a hug, and the three of us stood there for what felt like a small eternity, blanketed in a silence that was only punctuated by the occasional sounds of Mom's sniffles.

After a few minutes, Tanner pulled away and announced that he was going to go look for a squirrel he'd just seen run by.

"I have some peanuts in my pocket," he said solemnly. "And maybe he's hungry."

Mom nodded, and we watched Tanner head off. After a few paces, he broke into a run.

After a moment, Mom began crying again. I didn't know what to do. It felt awkward to be around a grieving person, especially my mother.

"It'll be all right, Mom," I mumbled.

"I've been a terrible mother," she whispered.

"No, Mom," I said, shaking my head. "It's okay."

"I'm the mom," she said, pulling a tissue from her pocket and blowing her nose. "I'm supposed to be the one who holds it all together. For all of you. And I haven't been able to do even that."

"You've done your best. I've done my best. We've all done our best. And it's going to get better."

"But your dad would have–"

"Dad would have understood," I said, "that you can't be perfect."

The words settled around us, and as they did, I realized that maybe I needed to take them into account too.

"I'm going to go sit in the car," Mom said with a sigh, turning away from Dad's grave.

Ten minutes later, I found Tanner sitting under a tree, gazing at a pair of squirrels, and together, we returned to the car. Mom already had the engine running and the heater going.

"Ready?" she asked.

We both nodded.

It wasn't until we'd pulled out of the parking lot that I realized I'd been so busy comforting my mom, I hadn't had a chance to say anything to my dad. I still wasn't sure that he could even hear me. I wasn't sure what I believed. But once again, I'd failed him.

chapter 21

There was a message on the machine from Logan when we got home.

"Sorry I missed the cemetery," he said, his voice sounding slurred. "I'm still out with Sydney. See ya later."

Mom hung up her coat and began sorting through a stack of mail.

"Mom?" I said, biting my lip. I'd always kept up the unspoken sibling rule of honor by not telling my mother if I saw Logan drinking or smoking at a party, but the fact that he sounded drunk at four on a Sunday afternoon worried me. "Doesn't Logan sound kind of . . . funny?"

"It's been an emotional day for all of us, Lacey," she said, sighing. "I'm sure he's shed a few tears of his own."

That wasn't what I meant, but there was no point arguing with her.

Later, after dinner, I decided to go for a run. I needed to get out. Logan still wasn't home, and Tanner and Mom were watching some show about pandas on Animal Planet.

The night had turned cold. The rain that had started just after we got home from the cemetery—and had dried up another hour after that—had brought with it a chill in the air that hadn't been there before.

As I set out at a slow jog, I wasn't quite sure where I was going at first. I just knew that I needed to be alone.

As I ran, my feet carrying me farther from home, I thought about my dad, I mean *really* thought about him, for the first time in a very long while. It was easier not to think about him most of the time. I'd stopped letting the memories in. I'd stopped talking to him in my head, pretending he could hear me. I'd stopped looking obsessively at his pictures. A little part of me *wanted* to forget his face, his warmth, his deep voice, his lopsided smile, because it would be easier that way, wouldn't it?

And now he was back. Seeing his gravestone for the first time since the funeral had brought it all home. No matter how fast I ran, I couldn't escape the reality that he was gone.

My feet carried me the two miles to the cemetery. I didn't even stop to consider that I shouldn't be coming this far by myself after dark. It was like I was numb to everything: good judgment, logic, even the bitter cold that was seeping in through my double-layered sweatshirts. I patted the pocket of my sweatpants and felt the familiar shape of my cell phone.

Slowly, I made my way up the shallow hill until I could see my father's headstone emerge from the darkness. A moment later, I stood in front of it, gazing down for the second time today at his name, the year of his birth, the year of his death. My knees suddenly felt weak, and I reached for the headstone to steady myself.

"Hi," I said softly. "I'm sorry." My voice didn't sound like my own. In fact, it took me several seconds to register that the voice was mine, that I had spoken the words aloud instead of just thinking them. I took a deep breath and repeated the words a little louder. "I'm sorry," I began again, "for not always being a very good daughter. I'm sorry for all the fights we had. I'm sorry for the times you told me I was being a brat and you were right. I'm sorry for the times I yelled at you that I hated you. I never meant it. Not once. I wish I could take them all back."

My knees were growing weaker; my legs felt like jelly. My hand still on the headstone, I eased myself down on the dead grass. The rain had left the ground damp, and I could feel it seep through my sweatpants almost immediately. But I didn't care.

"I'm sorry for that morning," I went on. "I'm sorry I took so long getting ready, just to bug Logan. I'm sorry I took my time coming downstairs. I'm sorry I thought that was funny. I'm sorry I thought it wouldn't matter."

My heart was pounding quickly now, and that familiar icy feeling was back. But still no tears. "I'm sorry that I didn't look up sooner. I'm sorry that I saw the SUV but didn't say anything. I didn't have time, but I should have. I should have thought more quickly. I'm sorry I blacked out. I'm sorry I couldn't hold your hand. I'm sorry I couldn't save you."

I felt short of breath. The words were coming faster, piling out on top of each other. "I'm sorry it was you and not me." I heard myself say the words, and they surprised me even as they came out of my mouth. I hadn't known I'd felt that way until that very moment. I hadn't let myself think about it. But if I'd been just a second faster, if I'd snapped my seat belt right away instead of giving Logan a hard time, if I'd spent one less stupid second in the bathroom making sure my lipstick was just right, then we would have been several inches farther along the road, and the car would have missed Dad and plowed into me in the backseat instead.

Maybe that was the way it was supposed to happen. Maybe I had cheated fate.

"I'm sorry I haven't done better," I went on. The more things I apologized for, the more miserable I felt. "I'm sorry I haven't done a better job of taking care of everyone. I don't know how, sometimes, Daddy. It's really hard. But I know it's what I have to do. I know I have to do that for you. And I'm sorry I haven't done better. I promise to try harder."

I sat there, staring at his headstone. I wasn't sure what I was waiting for. But there was only silence.

"I'm sorry," I said again. I leaned forward and felt the cold marble of the headstone on my forehead. The cold was cutting into me now, but I didn't care. I fervently hoped that somewhere, my dad could hear me. "I'm sorry. I'm sorry. I'm sorry."

I repeated the words, again and again, until the pain in my chest was so great that I couldn't take it anymore. I couldn't feel my dad's presence. Not at all. I realized I was talking to myself.

I stood up, cleared my throat, and touched the gravestone once more. I dusted what dirt I could off my sweats and, with one last, long glance, turned away.

• • •

I walked toward the parking lot and saw a vehicle parked in the far corner of the lot, in the shadows. Who would be here this late? My heart hammered and I reached for the phone in my pocket. I shouldn't have come here. What if I had gotten myself into a dangerous situation?

And then, as I tentatively walked closer, I suddenly recognized it. And the person leaning against it, watching me approach.

Sam straightened up and began walking toward me at the exact instant I realized it was him.

"Hi," he said as we approached each other.

"Hi," I said, staring up at him as the distance between us closed. We were standing face to face, under a dim puddle of light from a flickering streetlight. "What are you doing here?"

"I went to your house, and your mom said you'd gone for a run," he said.

"But how did you know I'd come here?"

"I couldn't think of anywhere else you'd go. Not today, anyhow."

"Oh" was all I could manage. There was something about realizing how well he knew me that made my stomach flip. We stared at each other for a moment. Then I asked, "Did you rake the leaves in my yard this morning?"

"Yeah," he said.

"Why?"

He looked a little embarrassed. "It was important to you. It was a memory you had with your dad."

"You can't bring him back, you know." My voice sounded angry, and I wasn't sure why I was directing any of that toward Sam. But my stomach was all tied up in knots. "Just by raking leaves. He's gone."

"I know."

I looked away. "It's not fair."

"What's not fair?"

I swallowed hard. "Your dad loved you enough to stay. My dad . . . didn't. And sometimes I hate him for it."

There. I had finally shown Sam the last of the cards I had kept so close to my chest, the cards I hadn't even known were there. How could I hate my father, even a little bit? Surely it made me the worst person in the world. And now I'd shown Sam just what a despicable human being I really was.

He stepped forward and pulled me into his arms.

I was startled, but I finally let myself relax into the embrace. I tentatively wrapped my arms around him and returned the hug. He responded by holding me tighter, like he would never let go.

"It's going to be all right, you know," he whispered, ruffling my hair with his breath.

I opened my mouth to tell him he was wrong, but before I could even get a syllable out, he had put his hand gently over my mouth.

"Stop, Lacey," he said. "Stop always having to be so tough. Just have some faith."

"Sam," I said after a minute, "I still haven't seen a rainbow." I paused and added, "I've looked."

Sam stroked my hair. "Maybe you haven't really needed your dad yet," he said. "You know, it's okay to hate him a little. He *did* leave you, even if he never would have wanted to, Lacey. But it made life hard for you. Life is *still* hard for you. He'd understand."

"How can I feel like that and still love him so much?" I asked in a small voice.

Sam was silent. "I think," he said, "that's exactly what love is."

Sam's words, and the fact that he was finally absolving me of everything while he held me tight, made something inside me snap. I didn't even know it had happened until I felt the first tear roll down my right cheek, followed soon after by a single tear from the other eye. And then, they were coming like a deluge, one after another, tears falling from eyes that had been dry for a year.

"You're crying," Sam said, leaning back. He looked concerned. He reached in to gently wipe a tear away.

"I know," I said. I reached up and touched my cheek. "I know." And for the first time that day, I smiled.

We stood in the middle of the cemetery parking lot for

a long time, under the glow of the flickering light, enveloped in a dark silence. But I'd never felt so safe in all my life. I didn't want to move, didn't want to go back to reality.

And then, my cell phone rang, a sharp jangle that invited reality back in.

The spell was broken. I looked at Sam as I pulled away. I looked at the caller ID. *Mom's Cell.* I didn't know why she'd be calling from her cell instead of the home phone, but I knew she was probably wondering where I was.

I snapped my phone open. "Hello?"

"Lacey?" Her voice sounded frantic. I felt immediately bad.

"Mom, don't worry; I'm fine," I said quickly. "Sam's here with me, and–"

She cut me off. "It's Logan. There's been an accident. He's at the hospital. I need you to come right away."

chapter 22

We got to Plymouth Regional Hospital's emergency room in record time. Sam dropped me off near the ambulance bay and promised to be inside as soon as he parked. I dashed inside and wildly scanned the waiting room for my family.

I spotted them immediately. Mom was standing in the corner, looking disheveled, and Tanner was sitting in a chair, his head down, mumbling to himself. Sydney was standing several yards away, her face tear-streaked.

"What happened? Is he okay?" I demanded, running

up to them. All three of them looked up. "Please!" I snapped. "Is he okay? Tell me!"

"I don't know," Mom said. She appeared exhausted. "He's in surgery now. The doctors will be out to talk to us as soon as he's done."

I stared at her. My whole body felt cold. *Surgery. Doctors. An accident.* It was all so familiar.

"What happened?" Just then, Sam came through the doors of the waiting room and jogged over to me. I introduced him to my mom, who nodded vaguely. I glanced down at Tanner and realized that he had reverted to sucking his thumb, something I hadn't seen him do since those dark weeks after Dad died. "What happened, Mom?"

"Apparently, Logan was drinking," she said in a tight voice. "With Sydney." She glared at Sydney, who seemed to shrink under her gaze. "He took the keys to Sydney's car," Mom continued through gritted teeth, "and went out to drive around the neighborhood. To find the spot of your accident with Dad."

I felt tears in my eyes.

"He didn't come back for a while," Sydney cut in, glancing nervously back and forth between me and my mom. "So finally, I got worried and took my dad's car out to look for him. I found him on Old Port Road. You know, the one by the harbor that curves? I guess he took the turn too fast and hit a telephone pole."

Mom made a muffled sound and turned away. I sucked in a deep breath. Tanner curled up on the seat and closed his eyes, sucking his thumb more furiously now. Sam wrapped both of his arms tightly around me and squeezed.

"The police were already there," Sydney continued. "And the ambulances. They were just taking him away on a stretcher. That's when I called your mom."

"Did you see him?" I demanded. "As they were taking him away?"

I wanted to ask her if he had been conscious, if there had been blood, how he had looked. But she just shook her head. "They were already shutting the doors to the ambulance. I only knew it was him 'cause of the car. It's totally ruined. My parents are going to *kill* me."

In this moment, with my brother lying somewhere behind closed doors and possibly dying, *she was worrying about her car?* I wanted to wring her perky little neck with my bare hands. But Sam held on to me and murmured in my ear, "It's not worth it."

He was right. But I'd never hated someone quite as much as I hated Sydney right then.

An hour passed without any word. My mom paced for a while, then sat down, chewing so hard on her lower lip that it started to bleed. She didn't even seem to notice. Tanner's eyes glazed over as he continued rocking back and forth, sucking his thumb. Sydney sat several seats away from us, alternately staring at the wall and texting on her phone. The whole time Sam sat next to me, rubbing my back gently and occasionally whispering things like, "It's going to be okay, Lacey."

His words weren't much comfort. But his being there was. At least a little bit.

Finally, a doctor in pale blue scrubs came out of the swinging doors leading to the operating room. "Mrs. Mann?" he asked, scanning the waiting room.

My mom jumped up immediately. "Yes, that's me," she said. "I'm here. How is he?"

I was on my feet before I knew it, standing at Mom's side. Sam appeared behind me a second later. Tanner stood up and grabbed my hand. Sydney just sat there, staring nervously.

The doctor glanced around at our little group. "Logan's a very lucky young man," he said. "He's going to be fine."

I didn't think I'd ever felt so relieved in my entire life. My knees buckled a little, but Sam was there to catch me.

"He is?" Mom demanded, almost as if she didn't believe it. "Are you sure?"

The doctor still looked concerned. "Yes," he said slowly. "He suffered a concussion and several broken bones, but it appears his internal injuries are minimal, aside from the trauma to his liver. He should make a full recovery."

"Oh, thank God," Mom breathed. I could see tears glistening in her eyes as she turned to me and smiled. I could feel the tears in my own eyes too.

But the doctor didn't look as happy as we did. "Mrs. Mann," he said slowly. "It seems to me that we have a difficult situation here."

"What?" my mom asked, sniffling a little.

He cleared his throat. "Your son's blood alcohol level is quite high. I asked him some questions, as did the police, and it seems that this isn't the first time he has gone overboard with drinking."

"What?" My mom looked at the doctor blankly.

The doctor cleared his throat again. "I suspect he will have to deal with the legal ramifications of this incident. I need to strongly recommend that you get him into some sort of rehab program."

"Rehab?" my mother whispered.

"He's a minor, Mrs. Mann. This is extremely serious. He's very lucky that no one besides himself was hurt."

She looked down. "Today's the anniversary of his father's death," she said. "I don't know if he told you that."

"Ah," the doctor said. For the first time, he looked a bit sympathetic instead of judgmental. "I see. I'm sorry to hear that. Was it long ago?"

"A year ago today," my mother whispered.

"I'm sorry," the doctor said. "But this is a wake-up call, Mrs. Mann. Your son needs help."

I could feel my face flaming. I'd known my brother drank. I hadn't done anything to stop it. And he had almost gotten himself killed.

As if reading my mind, Sam leaned down and whispered softly in my ear, "Don't you dare go blaming yourself, Lacey Mann. You are *not* responsible for Logan. He did this on his own."

"But–" I started to whisper back.

"Not your fault," Sam said in a tone that left no room for argument.

The doctor was saying something to my mom about how Logan was under anesthesia and was a little groggy but could talk to her if she wanted to go in. The rest of us would have to wait until visiting hours tomorrow.

"After you see him," the doctor said, "the police will want to interview you. And I'd like to recommend a few rehab centers to you before Logan is released."

"Okay," she said in a small voice.

When the doctor disappeared, my mother crumpled to the floor. It was as if all her bones suddenly turned to jelly. "My God, my God, my God," she was murmuring to herself. I bent down and wrapped my arms around her.

"I'm sorry," I murmured. "I'm sorry I didn't do anything to stop him."

"My God, Lacey," she said. "It's not your responsibility. When did it start being your responsibility?"

"But–"

"Lacey, you're sixteen," she said. "You're not in charge of your brother's actions. It's my fault. I should have known."

I tried to reassure her that it wasn't her fault. But the words fell on deaf ears. Tanner hopped up from his chair and joined me and Mom on the floor. He put his arms around both of us, and the three of us sat there in a messy, crying heap.

"It's not anyone's fault," he said. My mom and I both looked at him. Mom sniffled. "You can only do your best. And you can either get upset about the past, or just plan on doing things differently in the future. That's what the Crocodile Hunter said, anyhow. In a show I used to watch."

"Thanks, Tanner," my mom said.

He shrugged and put his hands in his pocket. "Whatever."

• • •

Sydney's parents came to pick her up a little while later. To their credit, they didn't say one word about the car. Mom decided to stay at the hospital overnight. Sam offered to drive me and Tanner home, and my mom gratefully accepted.

Sam walked us to the door, and after I unlocked it and watched Tanner disappear into the house, Sam pulled me into a long embrace on the doorstep.

"Lacey, I don't know if this is the right time to say this," he said, "but I'd really like it if maybe you'd come meet my dad sometime."

I didn't know what to say.

"I mean, he's not himself," Sam continued. "He can't move one whole side of his body. And sometimes I feel like he doesn't even remember me. But he's still my dad."

I swallowed hard. I thought of all the things I'd said to Sam, all the selfish, warring emotions I'd felt over his father coming out of his coma. I thought about how I'd never see my dad again and about how lucky I was to not have lost my brother, too. I thought about what Tanner had said about how you couldn't live in the past and how you had to do things differently in the future.

Finally, I smiled. "I'd like that," I said.

"Good," Sam said, smiling back at me.

Then he kissed me goodnight.

• • •

My cell phone rang early the next morning, jolting me awake. I glanced at the clock as I dove for the phone: 6:55. My blood ran cold. Was it my mom, calling with bad news about Logan?

"Hello?" I answered breathlessly.

"Lacey?" It was Sam, and he sounded concerned.

I let out a huge sigh of relief. "I was afraid it was my mom and something was wrong with Logan."

"Oh jeez, I'm sorry," he said. "I just wanted to make sure you're okay."

I smiled. "I'm fine."

"Can you go to the window?"

I sat up in bed. "What?"

"I just want you to look outside."

A warm feeling spread through me. I wondered if he'd raked the leaves again. I got out of bed, pulled open the curtain, and looked down. But the leaf pile had dispersed in yesterday's rain, and no one had put it back together again. Early-morning sunlight beamed down on a front lawn that looked absolutely ordinary.

"I don't see anything," I said to Sam.

"Are you looking down?"

"Yes," I said, puzzled.

"Try looking up," he said mysteriously.

I did as he said, and right away, I saw why he'd called. I gasped.

Stretching across the sky and dipping down again in the distance was the prettiest, brightest rainbow I'd ever seen. It was just like the one in Sam's painting under the bridge.

"Oh my God," I breathed. I blinked a few times. I couldn't believe my eyes.

"Lacey," Sam said, "it's not even raining. Look. It's all sunshine."

I looked around. He was right. A few wispy white clouds floated by, but there wasn't a rain cloud, nor a drop of rain, in sight. There was no logical reason for there to be a rainbow.

"You can't tell me you don't believe now," Sam said. "Your dad's up there, Lacey."

I gazed at the rainbow. Then I craned my neck as far as it would go and strained to look up, my chin pointing heavenward. I smiled at my dad.

"Thank you," I whispered to Sam. "Can I call you later?"

We hung up and I stared at the rainbow for a long time. "Thanks, Dad," I said.

Then I sent Jennica a text. No way could I call her this early.

LACEYLOO321: call me when u wake up. miss u.

Then I dialed Mom's cell number.

She answered on the first ring. "Hi, honey. Is everything all right?"

"Yeah," I said. I took a deep breath, realized that it was the first time in a year I'd meant it. "In fact, I'm pretty sure that everything's going to be okay from now on."

epilogue

ONE YEAR LATER

The second anniversary of Dad's accident fell on a Monday, so we couldn't go to the cemetery until the evening, when we were through with school and Mom was home from work.

Sam had bowed out of the visit. He had gone with me to the cemetery over the past year, but today, he said, was for my family. He didn't want to intrude. And that was just one of the many reasons I loved him. He was always thinking about things like that.

His dad was doing a lot better. He liked to play board games, so Sam and I would get out Monopoly or Battleship and sit with him for hours. It sounded crazy, but it was one of my favorite things to do now. Tanner even visited sometimes, and he entertained all of us with his new jokes–he'd decided he might want to be a stand-up comic. He and Mr. Stone really liked each other.

Logan's car accident had been the wake-up call he needed. Because it was a first offense, he wasn't sent to jail, but he had to enroll in a program for teen alcohol abusers, which met twice a week. He had stopped partying, and he had started hanging out with his old friends Josh and Will again. He and Sydney broke up, and she had a brand-new BMW and a brand-new boyfriend.

Mom was finally closer to being her old self again. I still heard her sobbing at night sometimes. But those nights were a lot fewer and farther between. And her smiles at the dinner table were real.

As for Kelsi, Mindy, Cody, Logan, Sam, and I, we'd become even closer. A freshman named Amber had joined our group a few months earlier; her dad had died when she was five. And Jennica, who had broken up with Brian in January, sometimes came too. The group had decided that it would be okay, from time to time, if kids whose parents were getting divorced joined us.

Today my family met at the cemetery, just after the sun had gone down. The last remnants of the sunset–a few streaks of orange and fuchsia across a deep indigo sky–hung above us, lighting our way. I had a car now, an old Toyota, and I had driven Tanner and Logan. Mom came straight from work, trading her high heels for sneakers in the parking lot.

I came here more often now to ponder things. In fact, I'd come here just last week when I needed to think about a big college decision. I had asked Dad's advice. And in the silence, with the sunshine dappling through the trees around us and the wind stirring the leaves on the ground ever so slightly, I think I'd gotten it.

We gathered around his headstone and I swallowed hard. *Two years ago.* It was hard to imagine that it had been two whole years since my dad had smiled at me or hugged me or said my name.

My mom laid down a bouquet of roses and murmured something under her breath. They weren't words for us. They were for Dad. Tanner told a few jokes. He came to Dad's grave with me sometimes, and he told a few each time. And, he'd told me, he was pretty sure that Dad could hear his jokes wherever he was and was proud of him. I'd had to blink several times to stop myself from crying when he said that.

"I miss you, Dad," Logan said in a deep voice that was growing deeper by the day. He bent down on one knee and closed his eyes, and when he stood, there was a tear running down his cheek. He didn't bother to wipe it away.

I took a deep breath. "I have some news," I said. "I got a letter from Boston University yesterday." I paused and grinned. "I got in. I got accepted. And I think there's a pretty good chance I'll get that scholarship."

I had applied for a scholarship for children whose parents had died, sponsored by Kate's Club in Atlanta–the club that had inspired our group. Every year, the founder, Kate Atwood, chose a few kids to send through college.

You just had to write an essay about how your life had changed since your parent's death and what your plans were for the future. I had sat down to write an essay. Instead, I wrote twenty-two chapters. I couldn't stop writing. And Ms. Atwood had called to say that my story had moved her to tears, and she thought that with some editing, it could maybe even be turned into a book.

Mom was the first to hug me. "I'm so proud of you. And I know Daddy would be too."

I hugged her back and imagined Dad's arms also wrapped around me. I imagined what his face would look like, so full of pride and joy for me. And for a moment, I felt like he was there with us.

I'd wanted to tell my family first, but I could hardly wait to tell Sam later tonight. He'd been accepted at Northeastern. I knew we were young, and who knew what would happen in the future? But at least this meant we were going to be in the same city and we wouldn't have to deal with the whole long-distance thing. If we were meant to work out, we would.

Logan cleared his throat. "Well, I haven't heard back yet, but I applied to Suffolk," he said, naming a small university in the center of Boston. He'd taken a year off after graduation. "And I think my grades and SAT scores will get me in. So I guess we'll both be in the city."

Logan and I hugged. He drove me crazy sometimes, but we'd become a lot closer in the past year, and I couldn't imagine being far away from him. Plus, he'd probably need to hit me up for rides home to visit Mom.

Tanner was grinning. "This is perfect!" he announced.

"There's a comedy club in Boston that me and Sarah read about. And on Monday nights, they have amateur night for comics under eighteen. We're gonna work on our act. We should be ready by next fall. And you guys can come watch us and bring all your friends!"

I grinned back at my little brother. "You bet! You're going to have the biggest BU cheering section any comedian has ever had."

"Not to mention the biggest Suffolk cheering section," Logan added.

"*And* probably the biggest Northeastern cheering section too," I said, thinking of Sam. "Actually, it just sounds like you're going to have the biggest cheering section ever."

Tanner smiled from ear to ear. "Cool," he said.

Mom was looking at all of us, her eyes glistening. "Dad would be really proud of you," she said. "*All* of you."

As we walked away from Dad's grave that night, Mom held hands with my brothers, and I held Tanner's right hand, my own right hand outstretched. I was reaching for Dad. I knew he was right there with us, as much a part of our family as he had ever been. Just because we couldn't see him didn't mean he wasn't there.

Kristin Harmel is a longtime contributor to *People* magazine. It was while working on a *People* story that she got to meet Kate Atwood, who runs Kate's Club, an organization for grieving kids in Atlanta, which inspired this novel. Kristin lives in Orlando, Florida, and admits that she spends far too much time at Walt Disney World, which is just fifteen minutes from her house.

To learn more about Kristin, visit her Web site at www.KristinHarmel.com.